THE CASE OF THE MISSING LETTER

PRAISE FOR THE INSPECTOR DAVID GRAHAM MYSTERY SERIES

"Bravo! Engrossing!"
"I'm in love with him and his colleagues."
"A terrific mystery."
"These books certainly have the potential to become a PBS series with the likeable character of Inspector Graham and his fellow officers."
"Delightful writing that keeps moving, never a dull moment."
"This book is a MUST to read."
"I know I have a winner of a book when I toss and turn at night worrying about how the characters are doing."
"Totally great read!!!"
"Refreshingly unique and so well written."
"Alison outdid herself in this wonderfully engaging mystery, with no graphic violence or sex."
"This series just gets better and better."
"DI Graham is wonderful and his old school way of doing things, charming."
"Great character development."
"Kept me entertained all day."

"Wow! The newest Inspector Graham book is outstanding."
"Great characters and fast paced."
"Fabulous main character, D.I. Graham."
"The scenery description, characterisation, and fabulous portrayal of the hotel on the hill are all layered into a great English trifle."
"Inspector Graham is right up there with some of the icons of British mysteries."
"This is her best book, so far. I literally could not put this book down."
"Character development was superb."
"Please never end the series."

BOOKS IN THE INSPECTOR DAVID GRAHAM SERIES

The Case of the Screaming Beauty
The Case of the Hidden Flame
The Case of the Fallen Hero
The Case of the Broken Doll
The Case of the Missing Letter
The Case of the Pretty Lady
The Case of the Forsaken Child
The Case of Sampson's Leap
The Case of the Uncommon Witness

COLLECTIONS

Books 1-4
The Case of the Screaming Beauty
The Case of the Hidden Flame
The Case of the Fallen Hero
The Case of the Broken Doll

Books 5-7
The Case of the Missing Letter
The Case of the Pretty Lady

The Case of the Forsaken Child

THE CASE OF THE MISSING LETTER

ALISON GOLDEN

GRACE DAGNALL

The characters and events portrayed in this book are fictitious. Any similarity to real persons, living or dead is coincidental and not intended by the author.
Text copyright © 2018 Alison Golden
All rights reserved.

No part of this book may be reproduced, stored in a retrieval system, or transmitted in any form or by any means, electronic, mechanical, photocopying, recording, or otherwise, without express written permission of the publisher.

Cover Illustration: Richard Eijkenbroek

Published by Mesa Verde Publishing
P.O. Box 1002
San Carlos, CA 94070

ISBN: 978-1548506865

For my readers,
The Case of the Missing Letter is my love letter to you.
Thank you for all your support, kindness, and blessings. You have truly been the greatest gift.

"Your emails seem to come on days when I need to read them because they are so upbeat."
- Linda W -

For a limited time, you can get the first books in each of my series - *Chaos in Cambridge, Hunted* (exclusively for subscribers - not available anywhere else), *The Case of the Screaming Beauty,* and *Mardi Gras Madness* - plus updates about new releases, promotions, and other Insider exclusives, by signing up for my mailing list at:

https://www.alisongolden.com/graham

MAP OF GOREY LIBRARY

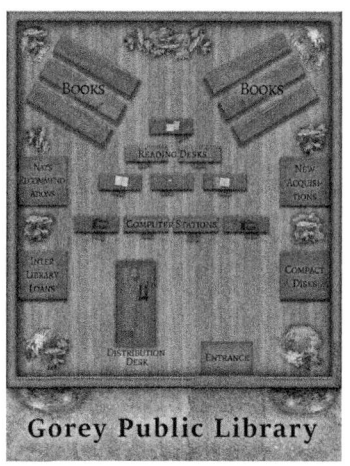

To see a larger version of this map, go to
https://www.alisongolden.com/missing-letter-map

CHAPTER ONE

DAVID GRAHAM TROTTED downstairs. The dining room was becoming busier by the week, but at least his favourite table by the window was still available on this bright Saturday morning. The White House Inn staff were busier than they had been since Christmas, welcoming and looking after new arrivals who had chosen to exchange the snow of Scotland or the dreary rain of Manchester for a few sunny days in Jersey. He took his seat and opened the morning paper, part of a reassuring and established routine he had been enjoyably following for the last six months.

As he settled into life on Jersey, Graham had followed the changing of the seasons as the island's surprisingly mild winter gave way to an even warmer and quite invigorating early spring. By mid-March, the island was once again beginning to look its splendid and colourful best. The spring blooms were out. Swathes of bright yellow daffodils and the unmistakable, bell-shaped blue hyacinth dotted the island. Economically, Jersey had also started to blossom. Most of Gorey's small fishing fleet had completed a month of refit and repair. Shortly, they would be heading out among the Channel Islands to catch lobster and oysters, or further into the Atlantic for cod.

"Good morning, Detective Inspector," Polly offered carefully. Before his first cup of tea, Graham could be sleepy and even uncharacteristically sour. Guesthouse owner, the redoubtable Mrs. Taylor occasionally reminded staff not to engage him in anything beyond perfunctory morning pleasantries before he was at least partially caffeinated. "What will it be today? Or are you going to make me guess again?"

Graham peered over his newspaper at the freckled twenty-something redhead who had become perhaps his favourite of the staff. "I have to say, Polly," Graham told her, folding the paper and setting it on the table, "that you're becoming something of a psychic. What is it now, four correct guesses in a row?"

"Five," Polly said proudly. "But on three of those days, it was that new Assam you were so excited about."

"True, true," Graham noted. "And I hope you'll agree it was worth getting excited over."

Polly shrugged. "I'm not really a tea drinker," she confessed. "But today I'm going to guess you're in... what do you call it sometimes... a 'traditional mood'?"

"I might be," Graham grinned. "Or I might be feeling spontaneous."

"Lady Grey," Polly guessed. "Large pot, two bags, sugar to be decided on a cup-by-cup basis."

Impressed, Graham raised his eyebrows and gave her a warm smile. "Precisely. I don't know how you do it."

Polly tapped her forehead cryptically and sashayed off to the kitchen to place Graham's order. Since arriving at the White House Inn, and with the enthusiastic support of the staff and Mrs. Taylor, Graham had taken sole "curatorial control" over the dining room's tea selection. He took this role exceptionally seriously. The kitchen's shelves were now stocked with an impressive array of Asian teas, from the sweet and fruity to the fragranced and flowery, with much else in between.

Lady Grey, though, was becoming Graham's favourite "first pot." It was often given the responsibility of awakening the detective inspector's mental faculties first thing in the morning. It was in the moments after the first life-giving infusion of caffeine, antioxidants, and other herbal empowerments that Graham's mind came alive.

One useful byproduct of his daily tea ritual was the ability to memorise almost everything he read. His knowledge of local events was becoming peerless. With the aid of the local newspaper, Graham stored away the information that Easter was two weekends away, and the town's churches were inviting volunteers to bake, sing, decorate the church, and organise the Easter egg hunts.

Also stashed away for future retrieval was the nugget that Gorey Castle's much anticipated "Treason and Torture" exhibit was about to open. The gruesome displays were only part of the attraction, however. Two recently opened chambers had, until their inadvertent discovery a few months earlier, contained an unlikely and entirely unsuspected trove of artistic treasures. The discovered paintings had mostly been returned to their owners or loaned to museums that were better equipped to display pieces of such importance. But, interest in the find was still high, and ticket sales had been, to quote the castle's events director, the ever-upbeat Stephen Jeffries, "brisk beyond belief."

"Lady Grey," Polly announced, delivering the tray with

Graham's customary digital timer which was just passing the three-minute mark.

"First class, Polly. And it'll be bacon, two eggs, and toast today, please."

"Right, you are." She nodded.

Graham put the paper aside and focused on this most pleasing of ceremonies. First came the tea, promisingly dark and full-bodied, tumbling into the china cup. Then came the enchanting aroma, an endless complexity from such a surprisingly simple source. Next would come the careful decision-making process regarding the addition of milk; too much would bring down the temperature, and as Graham liked to think of it, risked muddling what the tea was attempting to express.

Finally, he would add just the right amount of sugar. Graham had taken pains to instruct the wait staff to ensure that it was available in loose, as well as cubed form, so that he might more carefully adjudicate its addition. He tipped an eighth of a teaspoonful into the cup and stirred nine times, anti-clockwise. Some things, as he was so fond of reminding his fellow police officers, are worth doing well. He chose to ignore their barely suppressed eye-rolls.

Graham took a sip and cherished the added bergamot that complemented the traditional Earl Grey flavour. But then, contrary to his usual practice, Graham set down the cup. An article on page six of the newspaper was demanding his attention. The headline was *Our Cops are Tops*, and he read on with a quiet flush of pride.

After their successes in recent months, it goes without saying that Gorey has the most capable police officers on the island. Led by the indefatigable Detective Inspector Graham, the Gorey Constabulary has successfully raised the rate at which it solves reported crimes from twenty-six percent, one year ago, to forty-nine percent, today.

"For once," Graham muttered contentedly into his paper, "the media have got their numbers spot-on." It meant, he had observed proudly to his team the previous day, that anyone planning a crime in their small field of jurisdiction would know that they had a one in two chance of getting caught. "Splendid."

Moreover, the actual crime rate has dropped by sixteen percent in the last twelve months. This is surely cause to congratulate DI Graham and his team, but Sergeant Janice Harding was modest when asked for a comment. "The Gorey public have been enormously supportive," she pointed out. "We rely on their vigilance and common sense, and they've stood by us through some complex and challenging cases." The popular sergeant, who has lived on Jersey for nearly seven years, was referring to the conviction of former teacher Andrew Lyon, who began a seven-year sentence at Wormwood Scrubs in January. Gorey Constabulary also met with success after murder investigations at Orgeuil Castle and the White House Inn. It seems our "top cops" are equal to any challenge. Gorey is fortunate to have such a dedicated and dependable crime-fighting team.

"'Top cops.' Sounds like one of those ghastly TV reality shows," Graham grumbled. "But I'll take it."

CHAPTER TWO

MRS. TAYLOR WAS striding through the dining room in her trademark flowery blouse when she spotted Graham looking just a little smug. "Someone's been reading about himself in the paper, I see," she said with a smile.

"The whole team was mentioned, I'm glad to see," Graham said. His pride was hard to miss.

"Enjoy your moment in the sun," Mrs. Taylor said warmly. "You deserve it." She patted Graham on the shoulder and continued toward the check-in desk where a tall, blonde woman was quietly waiting, a single slender suitcase by her side.

Graham returned to the article. His two constables, Roach and Barnwell, were mentioned by name including a brief recounting of Barnwell's heroics in the Channel some four months before and his subsequent trip to Buckingham Palace to receive the Queen's Gallantry Medal. The article even contained the customary photograph of Barnwell showing off his award in the palace courtyard. He was accompanied by his mother who shared a remarkable resemblance with her son, but who looked like she couldn't quite believe where she was, who she was with, or why she was there. For his part, Graham couldn't have been more proud of his small team, who were admittedly proving very effective after a somewhat shaky start.

He quickly took another sip of tea before it got cooler than he liked. It was just occurring to him that Polly was a few minutes later than usual with his breakfast when Mrs. Taylor returned. This time she was not alone.

"Detective Inspector Graham, I thought you might like to meet our newest resident, Miss Laura Beecham." Graham stood automatically, setting down his teacup once more. He found himself being introduced to the woman who had been standing at the reception desk earlier. She had the bluest possible eyes and was even taller up close, within an inch of Graham himself. "Just arrived from... Where was it you said, Miss Beecham?" Mrs. Taylor asked.

"Down from London," Laura said, extending a hand. She had a city dweller's pale complexion, but her direct gaze, wide cheekbones, and petite upturned nose gave her an honest, girlish look. "Just fancied a change of scenery. Nice to meet you." She wore a small fish pendant on a simple gold chain and was dressed for travel in a comfortable maroon t-shirt and black stretch trousers.

"Welcome," Graham said, a little surprised by his own shyness. It was some time since he had met anyone quite so striking or indeed, his own age. "You'll be staying here at the White House Inn?" he asked.

Laura nodded. "At least for a while. I haven't really decided yet. I'm fresh off the boat, quite literally." She smiled.

"Our beloved Detective Inspector runs the local police station," Mrs. Taylor said, as though boasting of her son's recent acceptance into medical school. "You simply *must* read the article about our local boys in blue." She caught Graham's eye. "Oh, and girl, of course." She tapped the morning paper that lay next to Graham's cup and saucer.

"*Sergeant* Janice Harding is one of our most highly respected officers," Graham told Laura. He stood up a little straighter, "The article was very flattering, but we were just doing our jobs."

"I'm told Gorey is a very safe place," Laura commented. "Quiet."

Mrs. Taylor opened her mouth but closed it again. Although Laura was technically correct, and Gorey boasted an enviable safety record, one of the very few recent murders in the town had befallen a White House Inn *resident*. Mrs. Taylor had been about to mention it until she remembered it wasn't something she should draw attention to.

"I'm sure you'll be very happy here," DI Graham said.

"Are you looking for work?" Mrs. Taylor interjected, "or will you be relaxing during your stay, Miss Beecham?"

"Actually, I was lucky enough to find a job at the library," Laura said, still clearly surprised at her own good fortune. "I start there tomorrow. Can't wait," she added brightly.

"Splendid," Graham said. "It's a small place, but very popular. Their local history section is especially strong," he added. "I'll say hello if I see you there."

Mrs. Taylor had taken a step back to observe the effect of her well-intentioned intervention in DI Graham's social life. Her soft spot for the detective inspector was well known. As a professional, he was enormously respected, but Mrs. Taylor just plain liked him. She found him wonderfully thoughtful and courteous in an endearingly old-fashioned way that reminded her, more often than anyone else, of her late husband. It troubled her that such a fine man, still in his thirties and with no wedding ring to deter would-be admirers, was still living the bachelor life. She liked having him around, but she had been keeping an eye out for ladies who seemed to fit the bill: youthful, intelligent, well-read. And, of course, single.

Stepping forward again, she said to Laura, "Will you be with us long?"

"Just as long as it takes me to find somewhere more permanent, Mrs. Taylor," Laura replied.

"Ah, well now, I hear rumours that DI Graham is looking for an apartment in Gorey. Perhaps the two of you could share the flat-hunting burden?"

Graham leant toward Laura. "Mrs. Taylor is only moonlighting as a hotelier. She's actually a top-notch government spy." His little quip achieved the desired effect, and Graham's suspicion that Laura had a beautiful smile was entirely borne out.

"I'll remember to sweep for bugs when I get to my room," she whispered back.

"Now, there's no need to poke fun," Mrs. Taylor chided gently. "I'm sure everyone here would understand if you left us, Detective Inspector, but I hope you know that we'd miss you terribly."

Mrs. Taylor deserved plaudits for her persistence, Graham thought. "I'll be curating your tea selection for a few months yet, Mrs. Taylor. Still looking for just the right place." He turned to Laura. "Have you any idea what you're looking for?"

"Oh, no," Laura explained. "That's way down my list of things to do. Besides, I haven't even properly checked in yet." Graham saw that Laura's suitcase remained with Otto at the reception desk. It seemed that Mrs. Taylor, never one to miss an opportunity, had prioritised matchmaking over showing the new guest to her room.

"Well, it's been nice to meet you, Detective Inspector. I'm sure we'll meet again." Laura turned to Mrs. Taylor and an almost imperceptible flash of her eyes told the guesthouse proprietor that she'd been rumbled. This impromptu speed-dating interview was over. Mrs. Taylor shepherded Laura back to reception and then upstairs, but not before throwing a self-satisfied smile over her shoulder at Graham.

"For crying out loud," he muttered as he sat once more and refreshed his tea cup. But he found himself smiling, and not purely, if he were honest, because of the glowing newspaper article.

CHAPTER THREE

DON ENGLISH WOKE to the sound of his mother softly singing along with the radio. The room's blinds were open, and bright afternoon sunshine gave a warm lustre to the yellow tulips by Susannah's bed. Don shifted in the armchair and rubbed his eyes. He watched for a moment as his mother sang quietly, mumbling most of the words, her eyes closed, and a happy little smile on her face. It was something by the Beatles, but he didn't know the name.

"How are you feeling, Mum?" he asked. He pushed his heavy, soft bulk out of the chair with a groan and stood by her bed, flexing his left foot that had gone to sleep during his half-hour nap. "You've always liked this song, haven't you?"

Susannah was smiling contentedly to herself. Her eyes opened. She seemed not to take in her surroundings for a long moment, and when she finally turned to Don, there was a visible struggle in her eyes. Finally, she asked, "Play it again?"

Don sat on the bed and took her hand in his. He was

finding it remarkably slight and cool these days, her skin mottled with age and soft like an old parchment. "It's on the radio, Mum," he reminded her. "What's the name of the song?" he prompted hoping to focus her thought.

But it was too late, Susannah was focused on the tulips. "Who brought those?" she asked, gazing at them. "They're lovely."

"I did, Mum," Don replied. It could not have been anyone else.

"Oh, thank you, sweetheart," she said, just as she had an hour ago and twice yesterday. "You're always so good to me." Another song came on, something from the sixties that Susannah recognised, and she had her eyes closed again, humming to the chorus.

Don held her hand, feeling the tiny tapping of her fingers on his palm as she followed the beat. As the song ended, Susannah's eyes stayed closed, and her hand was still once more. He listened closely and found that her breathing was regular and slow. "You have another little nap, Mum," he said, kissing her forehead. "Going to find some coffee. I'll be right back."

St. Cuthbert's was a bright, airy place with the most thoughtful and attentive staff anyone could hope for, and certainly a huge improvement upon his mother's dreary existence at Kerry Hill. He had come to know two or three of the nurses who were competent and kind. The most senior of them, Nurse Watkins, was responsible for implementing day-to-day medical decisions regarding his mother's palliative care. After three weeks here, Susannah Hughes-English was reaching the end. Don caught the nurse as she left the reception area.

"Oh, hello Don, m'love. How's your mother today?"

"Comfortable," Don replied. "She's been singing along

with songs from the sixties again."

"That's nice," the nurse said. "Does she need anything?" Sian Watkins caring blue eyes and that wonderfully lilting Welsh accent always made Don feel better about this whole sad ordeal.

"I don't think so, but thanks. I'm just going to get some coffee, and I'll stay until eight."

"Right you are, m'love," the veteran nurse said, and gave Don's burly forearm a comforting squeeze before setting off on her rounds.

The atmosphere at St. Cuthbert's was pleasant and carefully maintained. Most of the conversations were hushed and private. Doors were closed quietly, and sometimes it felt as much like a small town public library as a hospice. Don reminded himself that this was not the emergency room or even a conventional hospital. No one would be rushed in for treatment and few resuscitation attempts would ever be made. This place, he knew full well, would be the final stop on his mother's long journey.

He took a sip from his cup. The machine in reception produced a highly caffeinated, dark-brown liquid that brazenly masqueraded as coffee. It would keep him awake, at least. Don sat in the reception area for a few minutes. A woman about his own age sat opposite him, her fingers quietly drumming on the leather handbag in her lap. She wore sunglasses and was dressed expensively enough to stand out.

"Waiting for someone?" Don asked, pleasantly. "A ride?"

She nodded. "My husband. We've been here all day." It had not, quite clearly, been an easy one.

"You'll be ready to get home, I imagine," he said.

"As soon as he's finished the paperwork." She glanced

around, but there was still no sign of her spouse. "It's mad that they don't allow smoking in here," she said, her fingers continuing their drumming. "I mean, it's not as if..." She left the thought unsaid. "I'm sorry."

Don was always wary of asking personal questions, but he wanted to think about something other than his own impending loss. "Is it one of your parents?" he asked. "I mean, who you're visiting?"

"My father-in-law. He passed this morning." She stated it as a fact, with little obvious emotion.

"I'm sorry," Don said. There was an awkward silence. He sipped from the brown plastic cup of coffee and asked, "Had he been ill for long?"

"A while. Alzheimer's," the woman said, the single word summing up a decade of struggle and sadness. "A blessing, in the end. You know?"

Don nodded. "My mother is here. Bone cancer," he said, the words feeling harsh and unwelcome as always, "but her dementia has become a lot more advanced recently. Doesn't remember anything from the last few years."

"But her memories from fifty years ago are clear as a bell, right?" the woman speculated.

"Right," Don said. "She can still sing all the old song lyrics, but she forgets where she is.

Don couldn't make out the woman's eyes behind the sunglasses, but her body language seemed vaguely sympathetic. A moment later, her husband arrived, looking red-eyed and pale. "Okay, dear. We've done everything we need to," he said, his tired whisper only adding to the subdued atmosphere. The woman stood and graciously shook Don's hand before leaving.

He finished the dreadful coffee before it could cool any

further and returned to his mother's room. She was snoozing, but the armchair squeaked as he sat, and she woke. She looked at him, blinking over and over. "Don!" she grinned. "My sweet boy. Where did you come from?"

He was learning to let these comments go. "How was your nap, Mum?" he asked, taking her hand again.

"You know," she said, "I wish your father could be here. He's so busy." Susannah shook her head slightly. "Busy, busy, busy."

Again, Don held his tongue. He could have reminded his mother that his real father had walked out on them over forty-five years before, but he knew she meant that self-serving old crook, Sir Thomas Hughes, her second husband, the man she had insisted he call, "Father."

"He was such a good sailor," Susannah said, out of nowhere.

"Yes, Mum," Don said. He was used to these *non sequiturs*, part of a fragmented commentary on the home movies playing in his mother's ailing mind. Three weeks ago, she was still remembering recent events, but now, the only memories that surfaced were those from her earlier life, the seventies and before. It would not be much longer before she would forget who Don was completely. The thought made him shiver.

"The *Gypsy Dancer*," Susannah recalled. "Thirty-six feet long. Our home for two wonderful weeks."

"Where did you go, Mum?" Don asked. The nurses said that it was good to keep her talking during these more lucid moments.

"All over," she said with a gleeful little laugh. "Mexico and Jamaica, lots of little reefs and inlets. Two weeks and then back to San Marcos." She sighed and her eyes grew misty. "We were inseparable back then. Before everything."

CHAPTER FOUR

DON FROWNED. HIS mother seldom mentioned her relationship with Sir Thomas Hughes. Back when Don was a teenager, his mother's marriage had deteriorated badly enough to prompt a serious nervous breakdown. He had barely spoken to the industrialist again after Thomas's decision to commit his wife to an "in-patient care facility." Don had known immediately what the place truly was: somewhere for the broken-minded to be kept safe and for a small minority of fortunate patients, nursed back to health. In his mother's case, the bumbling of the doctors and the grim, hopeless atmosphere had made her mental state worse. Susannah had attempted two disastrous spates of "care in the community," and after that, made her home at Kerry Hill for nearly forty years, right up until her final transfer to St. Cuthbert's.

"What was it like before everything, Mum?" Don asked.

"He was always busy, busy, busy," she said again. "Meetings and travelling and managing his factories. You know," she continued, "he built four factories from *nothing*." She held up four pale, slender fingers. "Just like that!" she marvelled. "*Thousands* of people. All depending on him. Busy, busy, busy."

Don decided that silence was the most prudent option. He had never felt anything but hatred for Thomas Hughes. Not only had the man condemned his mother to an asylum, but he'd also wrecked Don's life. As an angry, sidelined stepson, he was banished to the care of his elderly, uneducated maternal grandparents when his mother was hospitalised. They could barely read. Life with them had been tedious and limited. He had felt like a burden.

Hughes had granted Don a stipend, but it dwindled to a pittance that ensured that he would have no degree, nor any of the world adventures that were Susannah's dearest wish for her son. Instead, his adolescence unfurled in a fug of cigarette smoke, beer fumes, and betting slips.

Now, Don held his mother's hand and let her carry on, her hoarse little whisper almost painful to hear, but it was far better than what would come later. Don dreaded even the idea of that final silence and pushed the thought away every time.

"Sometimes he wouldn't get up from his desk until two or three in the morning," Susannah was saying. She tapped Don's hand with deliberate fingertips. "Writing and thinking and planning. Hardly ever had time for me. Busy, busy, busy. I wish he'd come to see me," she said again.

Don didn't remind his mother that Sir Thomas had succumbed to a heart attack seven years before. Instead, he reached for something positive to say. "You were good to him, Mum. A good wife." Hughes had had a busy, complex life, and Don knew that his mother had tried her best to be a good partner through the eight difficult years they were together.

Before her breakdown, Susannah had been a gentle,

sweet, kind person, and Don, whilst he didn't know for sure, always believed that Sir Thomas had done something to anger her, some transgression or lie that served to corrode her already fragile mind to the point where it snapped. On his darkest days, Don imagined Sir Thomas tormenting her, berating her, forcing her closer to the edge, and then calling for the "men in the white coats" once he'd finally tired of her despairing, tearful complaints.

"I used to watch him, you know," Susannah said after a pause. Her blue eyes twinkled a little now, framed by neatly combed, soft white locks.

"Watch him?" Don asked, at a loss once more.

"At his desk. That lovely antique desk he bought himself when his third factory opened. He used to sit there," she told Don, "until two or three in the morning."

"Yes, Mum." Don sighed. "You said."

"He loved reading that letter." She paused and turned to her son with an earnest expression. "You know, don't you? Thomas read it over and over but always in secret. He made me promise."

"Promise what, Mum?" Don said. "What did the letter say?"

"It was beautifully written," she continued, as if she hadn't heard the question. "Thomas was so proud to receive it. He never cared about all the terrible things people said. There was a photo of the three of us on the beach. Summer of seventy-two, it was. I wanted to put it up on the mantel, but Thomas said I couldn't. Oh, the colour of the water." Her eyes glazed over once more. "I *adored* that shimmering blue. Always so warm." She sighed. "So *warm*."

Don was racing to catch up, fearful that this moment of lucidity and revelation would pass all too quickly. "Where were you, Mum?" he asked.

But his mother was hazy-eyed, dwelling in her own memories. "Long, lazy days," she recalled with a sigh. "Just the three of us and his servants. They caught big, tropical fish off the stern and grilled them for us on the deck."

Servants? "Who was the third person in the photo, Mum? Where were you?"

Susannah shook off the daydream and frowned at Don as though he'd forgotten his own name. "*San Marcos*, silly!" she said. "He was so charming. And so very handsome in his uniform. 'A strong and wise man,' your father used to say. Thomas always hid that letter in its own little box inside his desk. Secret, secret, secret." She trailed off, her eyes beginning to close again.

Don was desperate to know more. Who was the wealthy, uniformed individual she was talking about? And what was so very *secret*?

"Mum, listen to me. Tell me about the letter."

Her eyes opened just a fraction. "Hmm?" she said, her voice tiny and plaintive.

"The *letter*, Mum," Don said, more loudly. "Tell me about the letter. Who was it from?" But Susannah was sinking back into sleep.

Don stared at his mother for a long moment, hoping she might jolt back to wakefulness. He knew she would have no memory of this fragmented conversation when she woke up. He took out his cellphone and quickly wrote himself a note, including the details he could remember. It all seemed important, although he couldn't put his finger on exactly why.

Nurse Watkins appeared at the door just as he was returning the phone to his pocket. She looked kindly at Susannah and moved to pull the covers up over the frail woman's shoulders a little more. "Has she been talking much?" the nurse asked quietly.

"Yes, a little," Don said. "But just fragments. Bits and pieces. I've been trying to make sense of it, but…"

The nurse nodded. "It's nearly eight, m'love, and you've been here all day. Why not get some rest? She's in good hands."

Don rubbed his eyes and gave the nurse a grateful smile. "She is," he agreed. "The best." He kissed his mother's forehead once more, and then he turned down the bedside lights before leaving her room.

As he walked across the rain-soaked car park to his battered old VW, as he drove home down the quiet A282, and for the rest of the evening, Don English thought about Sir Thomas Hughes and his writing desk. "Who was that other person, Mum?" he asked the walls of his basement apartment. There was no reply, but still he asked the most pressing of questions: "Why did this letter have to remain so secret?" Unable to sleep, Don went for a walk just after midnight, his scuffed brown shoes splashing slightly in the puddles. "Secret, secret, secret."

Back at home, he set his alarm for the next morning but then sat in his old armchair in the living room, sipping a glass of cheap whisky. He finally went to bed sometime after two o'clock, drained by events and bothered by his mother's cryptic reminiscences.

His phone woke him just after four. "Mr. English? It's Sian Watkins."

He was bolt upright in seconds. "What's happened?" he asked, but he knew the answer, even before the nurse's kindly, Welsh voice confirmed it.

"I'm so sorry, m'love. It was just ten minutes ago. She slipped away in her sleep."

CHAPTER FIVE

THE WALK FROM the White House Inn to the library was a good deal further than Laura anticipated. As she walked along the cobbled streets, she mused over the idea of purchasing a small car. Arriving with minutes to spare, she took a deep breath and stepped inside. She found herself in a spacious building that seemed larger on the inside than she had expected. The distribution desk was in front of her, to her left. She readied a pleasant smile and approached.

"Erm, hello," she said to the librarian, a petite woman with dark hair whose name badge read "Nat." She was slightly older than Laura. "I'm Laura Beecham."

"Oh, hi!" Nat replied. "Welcome to Gorey. Hang on a sec." Nat set down the pile of books she was holding and lifted the counter so Laura could walk through. "I'm Nguyen Ling Phuong, head librarian," she said, shaking hands.

"It's very nice to meet you, Miss... um, sorry, what was your...?"

"Please don't worry. Everyone calls me 'Nat.' Much easier. I'm from Vietnam originally."

"Nice to meet you, Nat." Laura smiled, a little relieved.

"Have you just arrived on the island?"

Laura nodded. "Just yesterday. All a bit of a rush, but I love what I've seen of the place so far."

"It's beautiful, isn't it? The weather's pretty good, by British standards anyway, and there's always something to do. I've been here for six years, and I wouldn't live anywhere else."

"That's great to hear. It's certainly a big change from London," Laura said.

"London? Oooh, London's too big! I grew up in a village. Two hundred people. Gorey is perfect for me. Come on, I'll show you around."

The library was a single large room with thick, old beams supporting its sloping roof. The rectangular distribution desk was nearest the door, with racks of CDs on the wall to the right and the interlibrary loans to the left. Past the distribution desk were four computer stations, and behind those, six reading desks sat at the centre of the room between rows of very tall wooden shelves full of books. Half a dozen readers were sitting at the tables, whilst others browsed the neatly arranged collection; sections labelled "New Acquisitions" and "Nat's Recommendations" stood against the left and right walls. DI Graham was right. It was a solid, fit-for-purpose library, one that any town the size of Gorey could be proud of.

"It's a nice space, isn't it?" Nat asked. "It was a church hall for a long time, until the council decided Gorey needed a library, back in the fifties," she explained. "Before that, the Germans used it as a garrison. When we dug the new garden out back a couple of years ago, we found all kinds of army buttons and pins, even the odd bullet, but no bombs, thankfully."

"It's very nice," Laura agreed. "You must like working here."

Nat shepherded Laura along the shelves, showing her the Dewey Decimal System and where the stepladder was stored. "One thing I really like," Nat confided, "is that there are very few *hassles*. The people here don't need much help. We get some questions about loans from other libraries, but mostly people just read the paper or a magazine, or check out some books. They keep themselves to themselves mostly. During the daytime, it's sometimes just me here, keeping things neat and tidy, whilst three silent, possibly sleeping, old men read copies of the *Racing Post*."

"Sounds idyllic," Laura said. "I've been looking forward to a quieter life."

Back at the distribution desk, Nat gave Laura a quick demonstration of the library's cataloguing software. It seemed simple enough, as did the interlibrary loan system and new library card and renewal procedures. "The only time," Nat warned, "that it gets a bit rowdy is right after the schools get out, between half past three and four."

"Rowdy?" Laura asked. She visualised hordes of uniformed teenagers rampaging among Nat's neatly arranged shelves.

"Well, we had to change our internet policy. I'll spare you the details. Just kids being kids, I suppose."

"I can imagine," Laura said. Nat printed Laura's new credentials and gave her a plastic ID badge that would be pinned to her top.

A patron approached the distribution desk with two novels, and Nat efficiently checked the books out. "New librarian?" the elderly man asked.

"First day," Nat explained. "I was just telling her how the place gets crazy when the school kids are here."

The man gave a gentle laugh. "It's the boys, mostly," he explained. "A pretty lady is always going to get those teenage hormones racing." Nat threw a paperclip at him, and the old man left with his books, chuckling.

"Bad boy," she said jokingly after him. "It isn't just the teenagers. You'll be finding that out for yourself. But don't worry," Nat smiled. "They know not to go too far. Good people here. Kind."

Laura spent a few minutes practicing "dummy runs" to learn the library's distribution software. Then, a pair of eyes framed with wire-rimmed glasses appeared just above the counter. "Hi," he said.

Laura blinked. "Oh, hello. How can I help you?"

"Got another loan request," the boy said. He couldn't have been older than nine.

"Sure," Laura said. "You'll be my first, so it might take a moment."

Nat appeared at her shoulder. "I'll help. Hey, Billy!"

"Hey, Miss Nat," the young man replied. He had straight-as-a-rod brown hair and a sprinkling of freckles across his snub nose. His eyes were hazel and framed by unusually fair, almost white eyelashes. "I think I'm onto something," he said seriously.

"Oh, really? Making progress with your moon project?" Nat asked, tapping briskly through the loan form; she knew Billy's details by heart.

"Yeah," he said. "I can prove there's still a prototype Russian moon lander orbiting the Earth!" he enthused. "Above our heads, right now!"

Nat showed Laura how to complete the form, and she typed in Billy's request for a book with a lengthy title available only from London. "Billy is passionate about space," Nat explained. "He's trying to figure out what happened to the secret Russian moon-landing project in the sixties."

Laura regarded the young man, whose eyes shone at the mention of his favourite topic. "Secret, huh? Didn't know they'd had a project like that." Billy gave her a quick look that was hard to read. Disbelief? Disapproval?

He launched, with the gusto known only to nine year olds, into an explanation of how the Soviet Union had almost bankrupted itself trying to race NASA to the moon. Four minutes in, Laura felt sure that Billy could easily give an hour's lecture on the subject, without notes, to an expert audience.

"Okay, Space Commander-in-Chief," Nat said, curtailing his spirited performance. "Laura has a lot of learning to do. Your book will be here in…"

"Ten to fourteen days," Billy finished for her.

"Indeed. And we'll notify you, as usual," Nat said. "Anything else?"

"Nope," Billy said, and headed off back to the Science shelves in search of more clues.

"Quite a character," Laura said.

"Billy? He's the smartest person in Gorey, in his own way," Nat said. "Unfortunately, his mother thinks books are a waste of time. I watched her chase him out of here once. You'd have thought we were offering him drugs or something, rather than a little knowledge and a safe place to hang out."

Laura watched Billy scouring the shelves, mouthing a Dewey Decimal number over and over to himself so he wouldn't forget. He found the book he was looking for and grinned merrily to himself. He scuttled over to a desk to begin reading. "That's sad," Laura said. "But at least he seems happy here."

"He's our best customer. I stopped charging him for inter-library loans six months ago."

"That's kind of you." Clearly the small library was, for many people, a storehouse of information, a community hub, and a place of refuge. And that reassured her. After all Laura had been through, it was exactly what she needed.

CHAPTER SIX
FIVE DAYS LATER...

DON STUMBLED DOWN the last two steps. He found his slippers at the bottom of the stairs, and frowned at the sorry state of his living room. Glancing at the clock, he saw it was lunchtime. Hungover or not, action was urgently needed.

He poured a large glass of cold water and swallowed four extra-strength painkillers. Stumbling slightly, he made the decision to fling aside the living room curtains and push open the windows. The daylight made him squint uncomfortably for the next few moments, but the fresh air revived him a little and helped cleanse the living room of its dismal, smoky aroma. As he waited for the kettle to boil for a pot of tea, he bustled about, cleaning off ash and bottle tops from the cracked glass surface of his old coffee table and setting out his blue plastic folder of notes.

"DESK," was the heading of one sheet. On this page, he had written out everything he knew about Sir Thomas Hughes' famous writing desk. There wasn't much. Digging through his brain, he'd managed to remember the desk's maker and roughly when Sir Thomas had acquired it, but his notes were absent a clue as to the most important detail: its location.

The next sheet of paper related to "MYSTERY PERSON." Don had little to go on except his mother's mention of San Marcos. He'd found the tiny nation on a map, nestled between larger neighbours in Central America, but he knew no more than that. His notes were largely speculative: *Rich? Playboy? Business associate?*

The third page was neatly entitled, "LETTER." He had already transcribed the notes he'd hurriedly tapped out on his mobile phone at the hospice as his mother slept that night. They remained the only record of her cryptic, confusing narrative.

Underneath each page of notes were some pictures and related articles photocopied from the library or printed from the internet. For now, the "Letter" pile was less substantial, but also less important. His top priority remained learning about the elusive piece of furniture that had been known in the Hughes family as the "Satterthwaite Desk" after its illustrious maker, Ezekiel Satterthwaite.

The furniture maker had been born to a cobbler and his wife in 1761, one of nine children. He had looked destined to follow in his poverty-stricken father's footsteps, but defying his working class roots, Satterthwaite built a reputation for designing fine furniture in rococo and neoclassical styles. His work had become highly sought after by the wealthiest people in Britain and Europe in the latter part of the eighteenth and early nineteenth centuries, and Satterthwaite's work now regularly exchanged hands for over a million pounds each.

In addition to having creative flair, Don learnt that Satterthwaite had a strong engineering bent. His furniture was robust as well as beautiful. He was a well-loved and kindly man who had a childish fondness for secrets. A signature whimsy was to occasionally, but not always, place compartments inside his pieces. He never announced their existence. As his reputation grew, it became a source of pride and excitement among those who owned his work to learn that theirs contained one of Satterthwaite's secret additions. Many others spent hours examining their commissions only to be disappointed. Many more were never sure either way.

An idea had formed in Don's mind. He wanted to locate the desk, but he had no earthly idea even where to start. Or at least he hadn't until eleven-thirty the previous night.

It had been the bitter end of the toughest and most despairing day Don had ever lived through. Susannah's funeral had been held at the tiny St. Mark's Church, a few miles from where she'd grown up. The small volunteer choir had outnumbered the congregation.

The priest made some heartwarming references during the service. There was no way of knowing if he said them at every funeral, but he seemed to have known Susannah a little. He had called Don the previous Wednesday, inviting him to speak at the funeral, but on reflection, Don had decided not to.

Someone from Kerry Hill was there, a man in a dark suit who spoke briefly with Don after the service and then left. There was Angela, an old school friend of Susannah's, who claimed to have visited her regularly at Kerry Hill, though Don couldn't ever remember meeting her. And there was Miss Pardew, who had been running the corner shop for decades. She told Don an endearing story about how a young Susannah had helped look after the store when old Mr. Pardew was losing his battle with heart failure. In all, they'd managed to say goodbye to his mother with dignity and sincerity, even if the loneliness she often felt in life was mirrored in death.

The silence in Don's living room in the hours after the funeral was utterly intolerable, so he'd laid out the complete contents of his drinks cabinet and methodically steered himself toward a state of oblivion. As midnight approached, there was a brief moment of clarity amidst the crushing depression and loss. Still able to hold a pen at that point, Don had roughly scribbled a word at the bottom of the "DESK" sheet. Now, in the light of the following morning, it took a little deciphering. The first letter was certainly a "P," but recognising the other letters was a struggle. Eventually, Don recognised the name. And it was one which, if he were lucky, could really open some doors.

He drank the tea he had made and rummaged in a couple of drawers looking for his address book. It hadn't been used since the days before mobile phones. Finally armed with the number, he tried to think back to when they had last spoken. Was it ten years? Twelve, probably. Don decided it didn't matter. The awkwardness of a Friday afternoon call following years of silence was trifling compared to the importance of his task.

The phone rang at length. Don looked out onto his dejected garden, finding that the weeds had truly taken over following a year of neglect. After eight rings, to Don's great relief, there was a voice.

"Prendergast."

Thank God. "Carl? Hey... It's Don English."

"Don?" There was a pause. "Ah, Don! Yes. Sorry," the man chuckled. Carl Prendergast was the Hughes family lawyer, a slight, wiry man with rimless round spectacles, and a spectacularly creased face. "How are you?" Prendergast asked, politely enough.

Hurting, lonely as hell, and probably still drunk. "I've seen better times, Carl. Did anyone give you the news about my mother?" Nobody had, of course, and so Don was obliged to recount her story once more: the steady decline in Susannah's memory during those last few months at Kerry Hill, the lazy, negligent staff, and then the peaceful three weeks at St. Cuthbert's when the nurses had made her comfortable so she could die with dignity.

"I'll be sure to tell the rest of the family," Prendergast said, after offering his condolences. "I'm sure they'd wish to keep your mother in their thoughts." *Yeah, right.* "Whilst we're talking, I should ask, is everything alright with the stipend?" There was a rustling of papers, evidence that Carl liked to keep things old-school. "No change in the account numbers, or anything?

"The money's fine," Don lied. It hadn't covered half of his bills even ten years ago, and the forty-year-old agreement didn't even provide for an inflation-based increase. These days, a month of Sir Thomas' generosity wouldn't have bought a bottle of whisky. Even the cheap stuff. "Actually, I'm calling about something else. I've got a question about one of Sir Thomas' possessions."

Carl clicked a pen. "Oh?" he asked warily.

"There was a desk. A rare collector's piece." Don picked up the best picture he'd found, printed from a website on antique furniture. "I'm probably going to say this wrong, and I can barely spell it, but the designer's name was..."

"Ezekiel Satterthwaite," Carl announced. "I know, it's a mouthful, isn't it? Beautiful piece, though. One-of-a-kind, hand-crafted, a stunning example of his work. What do you want to know about it?"

Don levelled with the lawyer. "What happened to it, Carl?"

"The desk?"

Don knew that this was not the kind of question the lawyer would be expecting from the estranged stepson of a wealthy, dead client. "That's right. Was it sold, or does someone in the family have it?"

More papers shuffled. "Don, would you mind holding the line for a moment? I've been the Hughes' family lawyer for thirty years, but I'm afraid I haven't memorised every last detail of the estate."

"Take your time," Don said, and took two more painkillers.

"Right," Prendergast said, moments later. "I've got the will, and the desk is near the top of the list, as you might imagine."

"Okay," Don said. He managed to keep his tone even, but he was trembling with impatience. His fingers rattled quietly on the scratched wooden surface of his coffee table.

"I'm just tracing the disbursement of assets," Carl explained. "Desk....desk.... where are you, desk?" he muttered, flipping pages. "Ah-hah! Right, yes. I remember now." Don waited, his nerves jangling. "It's on Jersey."

Don blinked hard. "Eh?"

"Yes, I remember now. Sir Thomas left strict instructions," Carl explained. "On his death, the Satterthwaite desk was to be bequeathed in perpetuity and without further family discussion to the Jersey Heritage Museum, where it was to be displayed in honour of the craftsman's connection with the Bailiwick of Jersey."

"Hang on," Don said, pinching the bridge of his nose. "Are you talking about *New* Jersey, in America?"

"No, no. The island near France," Prendergast clarified. "Satterthwaite's father was born on Jersey, and though the great man kept his workshop in London—logically enough, I suppose—he retired to the island and died there. Some time in the 1820s, I believe."

This was hardly the worst case scenario, but it wasn't a straightforward outcome, either. "So, it's on display at a museum? On Jersey?" Don asked.

"Indeed. Damned difficult to get it there, as I recall now. Your father," he began, "Sir Thomas, that is, felt strongly that the museum should have an important Satterthwaite piece. I haven't been to the museum, but one can guess that such an elegant, seminal work now has pride of place in their collection. Um, may I ask as to the nature of your inquiry?"

"Oh, you know, I was just wondering. I've been reminiscing and was curious as to what had happened to it."

A museum. Don would have given it odds of twenty-to-one. It was a real surprise to him that Sir Thomas hadn't kept the valuable desk in his family. Selling it for a quick profit would not have been out of character for his stepsiblings. This was an interesting outcome and also his first lucky break in a long time. "Okay, Carl. That's very helpful," Don said, scribbling notes.

"No trouble at all," Carl said. "Anything else I can help you with?"

"Actually, yes," Don said. "It's about the stipend…"

"Well, I'm afraid my hands are tied there," Prendergast explained. "You see, the agreement is binding, so any alteration has to be co-signed by…"

"Carl?"

"Er… yes?"

"Stop sending it."

"I'm sorry?" Carl said.

"I want you to stop paying it into my account. Send it to a dementia charity."

Carl was shuffling papers again. "Really? You're quite sure?"

Don considered for one more moment, but then couldn't resist. "Absolutely sure. Thomas Hughes was a liar, a cheat, and an all-round nasty piece of work. I don't want any more of his dirty money. Understand? Good." *Click.*

CHAPTER SEVEN

JANICE PUSHED open the double doors with her hip, holding one of them ajar with her elbow as she manoeuvred her way through. She held two coffees in front of her. They sat precariously in a cardboard tray. She hadn't shoved them far enough into their slots, and they were threatening to tip over. Adding to the threat of disaster, the strap of her shoulder bag was slipping down her arm. It was about to make the quick slide to the crook of her elbow, at which point she knew her efforts to keep the coffees upright would be in vain. She awkwardly sidled over to the reception desk as fast as she dare, scuttling like a crab, and lay the coffee tray down on its flat, solid surface. She heaved a sigh of relief.

"'Morning, Janice. To what do I owe this pleasure?" Constable Jim Roach asked, looking up at her from behind the desk, slipping his phone onto his lap and from there into the desk drawer. It had been a slow morning, and he'd taken advantage of the peace and quiet to catch up on yesterday's football results.

"Just thought I'd pop in, Jim. See how things are going. Anything interesting?"

"Nah, nothing really. I'm just catching up on paperwork. Bazza's out and about. He'll be back soon." Jim sipped greedily at the coffee Janice offered him.

"How was your Saturday night? How's things going with that nurse you were telling me about?" Janice grinned.

Roach opened a file on top of a pile in front of him and shrugged. "She's alright."

"She's more than 'alright' from what you told me," Janice pressed. "I didn't even know you liked blondes."

Roach looked up and smirked at her. "There's quite enough romance going on around here at the moment, wouldn't you say? How's things going with Jack?"

Jack Wentworth was a computer engineer. He provided digital forensic support to the constabulary when they needed it. He was also Janice's boyfriend.

Try as she might, Janice couldn't keep the flush from her cheeks. After a period of being single so long that it threatened to become permanent, Janice was beyond delighted to be regularly going out to restaurants, movies, and, most recently, the farmer's market with the handsome and thoughtful Jack Wentworth. The young man was proving to be cultured, well-read, and a gifted cook.

"Fine, just fine," she said. "He's a nice guy."

Roach chuckled and hummed the first measures of *Here Comes the Bride*.

"Wind your neck in, Sherlock," she said, regretting she'd ever brought up the subject of romantic entanglements. "I'm going to check in with Viv Foster whilst I'm here."

"Ah yes. Gorey's Mother of the Year," Roach muttered.

"I hope Billy's alright. He's hanging around the library

more these days. Viv left a message yesterday, but I didn't have time to call her back."

Roach continued to leaf through a report. "Welp, let's hope she's doing better."

"Yes, let's," Janice said, heading to her office. It was seldom that she received good news from the Fosters, whose paths had crossed hers several times over the six years she had been on Jersey. Ever since she'd found a three-year-old Billy snuggled up to his unresponsive mother, Janice had kept a concerned and proprietary eye on him. The image of the tiny boy patting his mother's face as he tried to wake her had never left her mind. Recently, Billy had complained of being bullied at school, but he was doing a little better according to his teachers. He was unbelievably smart but not very socially adept, and it was easy to imagine him falling afoul of those with more muscle than brains.

She dialled Viv Foster's number. "Hello?" It was Billy's voice on the end of the line.

"Oh, hello Billy. It's Sergeant Harding from the station. How are you doing?"

A big sigh came down the line. "Mum's not very well."

Janice knew that meant Viv was either drunk or high. At eleven-thirty on a Sunday morning, it could be either. "Okay, Billy. Is she asleep right now?"

"I can't tell. But she's breathing. She hasn't said anything for an hour or two."

High, then. "Alright, mate. You want to come here for a while?" Along with the library, the police station was a sanctuary for Billy. He felt a little uncomfortable "running to the police" when his mother relinquished her duties, but it was a safe place. Even at the library, he'd occasionally run into groups of older kids, and they just loved to tease him about his glasses, his mother, his penchant for reading and memorising facts, and his ungainly, uncoordinated movements. One tried nicknaming him "Puppet Boy" but it hadn't yet stuck.

"Er, no thanks. I'll stay with her for a bit longer."

"Okay, Billy. I'll call in an hour and see how you're doing, alright?"

"Yeah, okay," he replied. Then he whispered, "Should I take it away from her again?"

"No, lad. I think that'll cause more harm than good, don't you?"

"Yeah, you're probably right," Billy agreed. "I don't want her chasing me around again. And I've run out of places to hide the stuff."

Janice gave him some more words of encouragement. She bit down the urge to say much more, and hung up. There had been perhaps four of these calls over the past eighteen months, and each one left her feeling angry and despairing. As a police officer, Janice's instinct was to arrest Viv for possession of a banned substance and arrange for Billy to be taken into care, but she believed in keeping families together wherever possible. Billy's mother was an addict and utterly unreliable. Her own child had to take care of her and yet he loved her. So whilst Billy's was a far from ideal situation, Janice couldn't see that moving him to a foster home, most likely on the mainland, would be much better. Keeping him close, in a small place like Gorey, meant she and the local community could keep an eye on him.

As she put the phone down, Janice heard a lot of banging and clattering, accompanied by a significant degree of colourful language. She recognised the voice. "Oi, you. Watch your language," she called.

Janice stood and walked into the reception area. Constable Barry Barnwell was wheeling his regulation police bicycle into the back where they stored everything they wanted to keep out of sight from the public.

The area needed a good cleaning out. Tins containing an assortment of teas, biscuits, and coffee lay atop reams of paper. Next to that sat a toolbox that couldn't be closed due to the claw hammer and screwdriver haphazardly thrown into it. The floor space was largely taken up by a discarded desk and a file cabinet between which the Gorey police team had resorted to storing a couple of riot shields. Barnwell propped his bike up against the desk.

"There has to be a better way. It's like Piccadilly Circus in there," he grumbled. "Couldn't I just leave it out front when I'm off-duty? Or take it home? Trying to get a bike through those doors at the end of a shift is a nightmare."

"Had a good morning, Bazza?" Janice asked cheerily.

"Not especially, no," he replied. There was a mulish look on his face. Janice raised her eyebrows. Barnwell took it as a sign to air his grievances. "First, we lost at the rugby yesterday. Second, that new couple in the flat upstairs didn't invite me to their housewarming party. And third, they kept me up all night with the noise!"

"Why didn't you tell them to keep it down? You are the police," Jim asked reasonably.

Barnwell merely grunted before carrying on. "And then this mornin', old Mr. Golightly at number seven bent my ear off for a good fifteen minutes about his neighbour's trees blocking his view *again*."

"Neighbour disputes are the worst," Janice said sympathetically.

"You're telling me. Been going at each other for *five* years, they have."

"Won't stop until one of them's in their grave, mark my words," Jim said sagely.

"Well, I'm off down the pub." Barnwell started to unbutton his reflective jacket. "A pint and a Sunday roast will do me right."

"And a snooze, I reckon," Jim said.

"Yeah, that too. Ha, I'm cheering up already." Barnwell went to hang up his jacket and replace it with a beat-up leather jacket.

"Anything else to report before you go?" Janice inquired.

"Nope, all's quiet on the Western front. Everyone seems to be enjoying the good weather. A few tourists are around, but everything's pretty sleepy and uneventful. No trouble other than those bloomin' trees."

CHAPTER EIGHT

DON FELT LIKE a new man. In contrast to Shropshire's weather, which apparently hadn't yet received the springtime memo, Jersey was a riot of colour. Yellow, blue, pink, and white flowers lined the roadside and beamed from the window boxes and front gardens of the neat houses near the B&B he had chosen.

Although the denizens of BedAdvisor.com had insisted that the White House Inn was *the* place to stay in Gorey, their rates had been a little beyond Don's modest budget, and he'd already spent a small fortune hiring a car for a few days. Instead, he opted to stay at a townhouse owned by an elderly widow just off the main thoroughfare through Gorey. His landlady was obviously supplementing her meagre pension by letting out a spare room, but his accommodation was pleasant and the breakfast tasty and plentiful.

Don closed the wrought iron gate to the townhouse's postage-stamp-sized front garden and walked the few steps to his rental car. He settled himself behind the steering wheel and let out a deep sigh, pausing for a second to consider his plan. Leaning forward, he turned the key in the ignition. The car's engine started with a quick shake and a low purr.

Don easily pulled away from the curb, the hour being early and the streets of Gorey less than busy. He spun the steering wheel calmly as he made his way through the town's mostly empty streets. The drive to the museum was peaceful as he took the small roads out of town at a deliberately steady speed.

At around ten o'clock the previous night, Don had found to his surprise that he was further from home than he'd ever been in his life. Although his mother travelled extensively after meeting Sir Thomas, Don had never been invited on their luxurious Caribbean cruises or their romantic weeks hiking their beloved Rockies.

Yesterday, Don's departure from the mainland had involved six tiring hours of train journey and a nerve-wracking change in London. A headlong rush across town from Paddington to Waterloo had ensued, only for him to find that he still had another hour to wait for his train to Poole.

The ferry ride across the Channel, however, was a real joy. Leaving behind the smog and chaos of the capital, and the drab, nondescript port town from which he'd left England, Don revelled in the fresh sea air and spent most of the journey enjoyably wandering around on the deck. There was nothing like crossing a body of water to remind a traveller that they were arriving somewhere brand new.

In truth, Don was more than ready for a change of scenery. Everything in his life and everything about it reminded him of his mother, so the decision to head to Jersey had been an unusually decisive one. Within an hour of his call to Carl Prendergast, he found himself staring at a half-empty whisky bottle on one hand, and his growing pile of research notes on the other. "Bugger," he said to the forlorn living room. "I'm off." It had likely been the only time in his life that he had possessed enough mettle to make a snap decision and carry it through.

Don parked the tiny hire car at the museum. He was early. It didn't open until midday on a Sunday. He took a walk around the area whilst he waited. The museum building was a large, ostentatious house with a plaque inset into the sandstone façade. The plaque announced that the building had been built in 1613 and was the original home of John Cateshull. Don presumed he was a local wealthy man of note, but in whom he wasn't sufficiently interested to delve further. The house was located on a quiet, expansive, and verdant part of the island, about a mile from Gorey itself. He could see the Gorey Grammar School playing field beyond the house's grounds on one side, and there was a large park on the other, complete with a bandstand and duck pond.

His plan, so far as he actually *had* one, was to merely lay eyes on the desk and try to judge what might be required for him to closely examine it. He meant the masterpiece no harm whatsoever, but his suspicion, fanciful as he told himself it might be, was that it may just contain something very meaningful indeed.

Don dearly wanted to fill in the gaps of his mother's mysterious story. Who was this wealthy individual she had holidayed with? Who wrote the letter she had talked about, and what did its contents contain that were so secret? Don felt sure the Satterthwaite desk was the key to answering these questions and besides, travelling down here to Jersey and working on this mystery were all a *lot* more fun than sitting on his couch at home, trying to ignore the ceaseless allure of the scotch bottle.

When it opened, Don found the entrance to the museum exceptionally grand. Converted to its new function after a lengthy funding drive, the house now acted as a display space for artefacts related to Jersey's history. A large chandelier sparkled above a hallway lined with paintings of Jersey luminaries and leaders, none of whom Don recognised.

He paid the entrance fee and walked into the main display space, which was the former ballroom. Don's shoes tapped crisply on the highly polished wooden floor. More portraits and works by local painters adorned the walls, and in one corner sat a beautiful, jet-black grand piano, a storied possession of the house's former owners, according to a sign mounted on a music stand in front of it.

There was another musical instrument, a *clavichord*, and several sculptures crafted from local stone. But, Don noted, there was no desk.

The ballroom led out into a three-room suite that occupied the back of the house. There were mannequins wearing ball gowns and wedding dresses, displays of military medals and ceremonial swords, signed first editions of classic books Don had never read or even heard of, and a large, framed, nautical chart of the waters to the east of Jersey.

Frustrated, Don quietly muttered, "Come on, come on, where the hell is..." And then he saw it, sitting on its own, surrounded by red rope under the back window. It stopped Don dead in his tracks.

CHAPTER NINE

SIR THOMAS HAD firmly prohibited all of his children from entering his private study, so Don was seeing the Satterthwaite desk for the first time. He had never suspected that it might be so *beautiful*. It wasn't just the wood tone, which struck a balance between formal and playful, between depth and sheen. And it wasn't merely the inlaid mother of pearl, which gave this singular piece of furniture a crystalline glimmer as the dark and light swept alongside each other in sumptuous, elegant curves. It was also the *shape*, the very proportions of the desk. It was a geometric perfection, conceived perhaps by a master mathematician but then realised in wood and leather and semi-precious stone by a consummate professional at the very height of his powers.

Don stared, slack-jawed. This was, he tried to remind himself, a *desk*.

Four sinuous, delicately feminine legs, so slender as to be unlikely, supported a broad, glass-smooth surface made, quite obviously, from a single length of the highest quality timber. There was a large, central drawer, flanked by two others, all with glinting, filigreed handles in solid brass. The sides were adorned with carvings so detailed and careful that they could almost have been etchings. The symmetrical blossoms, captivatingly three-dimensional, spoke of many dedicated, painstaking hours of work.

The accompanying booklet described the Satterthwaite desk as, "perhaps the perfect synergy of form and function," a description that Don found somewhat overripe, but admittedly, only a little. The museum was proud of its most spectacular acquisition, and with good reason. It was, without exception, the most remarkable piece of furniture Don had ever seen. There was just one problem. After ten minutes of careful reconnaissance, he concluded that there was absolutely no way *whatsoever* he would be getting anywhere near it.

The red rope was not simply an ornate deterrent to keep visitors from touching the desk. Discreetly taped to the floor underneath it was a thin, black wire that would assuredly trigger a noisy alarm if anyone crossed it. And there were *four* cameras in the room, as well as a permanently stationed security guard whose solidly muscular build would deter most would-be transgressors.

Don asked for and received permission to take some photographs. He took just enough, he hoped, to avoid arousing suspicion. There were no switches, catches or buttons on the exterior, and he obviously couldn't crawl on his knees to view the desk's underside without attracting unwanted attention. Whatever Sir Thomas Hughes' secrets might be, they would remain hidden for the time being. With frustration threatening to bleed into his behaviour, Don hurriedly took his leave.

Outside, spring was flooding the park and the school field next door to the museum with brilliant sunshine. Don breathed in the air, so different from back home, so much more *nourishing*, and then sat in his car with the windows open to digest what he had seen. The desk was a marvel, an absolute treasure. But security was tight. Accessing the closely guarded desk and searching for a secret compartment was, undoubtedly, going to be a three-pint problem.

He started the car and drove around the island for a couple of hours, partly to clear his head, and also to enjoy the peaceful scenery in Jersey's spring sunshine. With each passing mile travelled, he felt the stress and depression of the past few days leave him like a fog lifting on a spring morning. He found his thought patterns shifting as his mood improved.

He took a back road through a quiet village with a bright, glistening green. In the middle of the grass stood a memorial to the village's war dead. He thought carefully. The search for the letter was providing him with something to *do* in the quiet, sullen days after his mother's funeral.

As he continued down the country lanes, tall grasses serenading the car from both sides of the road, he realised that there was a dark side to his motivation for finding the letter, however. Certainly, it would be satisfying to come to a greater understanding of his mother's life with Sir Thomas, their trips abroad, and their associations, but there was a suspicion in Don's mind that the letter may reveal some information, some dirt on Sir Thomas Hughes.

Don considered his mother's treatment at the hands of her husband to have been cruel and inhumane whilst the rest of the family had stood aside. They had been complicit. If they were embarrassed or even scandalised in some way, it wouldn't bother him a bit. Whatever secrets the letter may expose, he wasn't above gaining some measure of revenge for his mother's and his own unhappiness at their hands.

Don slowed before turning into the car park of a quiet country pub. Another thought occurred to him. It was something his mother had stated—about the "terrible things" people had said about the author of the letter. "What was all that about?" he asked the interior of his hire car as he killed the engine.

Don ducked as he passed through the doorway of the pub into the deep, dark interior. Outside, the quaintly named *Frog and Bottle,* with its whitewashed frontage and tiny windows, had offered the prospect of a wonderfully varied selection of beers. Don found the promise kept as he perused the chalkboard on the bar. But before ordering a pint to go with his sandwich, he stopped himself short. He would drink no booze, no whisky, no wine, and none of the dozen items on the beer menu he was anxious to try, until he finally had the letter in his possession. That would be reason for real celebration.

CHAPTER TEN

CONSTABLE JIM ROACH jogged into the reception area carrying his football boots in one hand and his gym bag in the other. "Thanks so much for this, sir," he said. "It's the last but one game of the indoor season, and we're playing the Civil Servants again. One more win and we'll be confirmed Division champions."

DI Graham cut a slightly incongruous figure behind the reception desk, dressed in his white shirt and brown blazer instead of the customary desk officer's police blue. "Go ahead and grab yourself a hat trick. I only hope you don't get spotted by some talent scout and offered a contract by AC Milan. I don't know what we'd do without you."

Roach acknowledged the compliment with a nod. "Old Mrs. Hollingsworth has called in again. A suspicious character, she says. I'll drop by on my way. Check it out. I'm sure it's nothing. It never is," he said.

"Okay, let me know if anything changes."

Roach grinned and headed to his recently acquired, third-hand car. If he were lucky, he'd arrive in time to warm up before the game. He was the team's first choice midfielder, but he was useful on the wing and even played up front when pressed. Roach was looking forward to giving their pen-pushing opponents a good thrashing. First though, he'd attend to Mrs. Hollingsworth's call. It shouldn't take too long.

The man observed the library through a side window. He could see the woman he was looking for. For a library as small as this, it was taking Laura a long time to tidy it up. She had put away newspapers and stacked some other things that he couldn't see on the shelves. Then she busied herself around the distribution desk and moved some more piles of books from place to place, checking items off a list on her clipboard. She turned off the library's lights, section by section, until only those above the distribution desk remained lit. She would be out soon. He was ready for her.

Tires crunched on the gravel of the library's short driveway. A car was approaching. The man swore colourfully under his breath and headed along the side of the building and into the park where he sprinted a short distance. He was lost in the shadows within moments.

He turned and looked back. The car had stopped, and a young man had got out. He recognised him as one of the coppers he'd familiarised himself with when he arrived on the island. The policeman nosed around for a moment, shining his flashlight into the bushes and around the back of the building, but he didn't come close to illuminating him before returning to his car and driving off. The man turned his attention back to the library.

Laura appeared to have seen and heard nothing, finishing

her tasks just as the clock struck seven. All was quiet and dark. She came outside with an armful of books and made her way over to her car. When the library door slammed shut behind her, she stopped suddenly and raised her face to the sky, but after hesitating for a few seconds, she continued over to her hatchback and deposited the books in the back. She climbed in behind the steering wheel and drove away.

The man edged back toward the library car park and watched her leave. Foiled and frustrated, he sat on a bench in the park, listening to an owl hooting in the distance and cursing his luck. He made sure that his silenced pistol had its safety on, deep in his jacket pocket, and then sent a brief text:

Found her, getting closer, all under control. Will update tomorrow.

The man sighed and headed back to his digs, a simple B&B in the town.

It hadn't been a difficult decision for Graham to head to the station after his Sunday dinner. His evening options basically boiled down to sitting around in the dining room or on the terrace of the White House Inn, where there was every chance Mrs. Taylor would bring over at least one likely female companion to entertain him. To escape that, he occasionally took himself down the pub, but that was something, with his history, he was keen to avoid. This evening, he'd determined that if he were going to be sitting, he may as well catch up on some paperwork at the office. Graham was leafing through a file when a figure appeared at the lobby doors.

"Er, hello?" she said tentatively, as though uncertain anyone would be there.

Of all the gin joints in all the world... Graham gave her a welcoming wave. "Good evening, Miss Beecham."

"Laura, please," she said, huffing a little as she calmed herself down.

"What can I do for you, Laura? Is everything alright?"

"I'm very relieved you're here. I'm afraid I've gone and done something rather silly."

Graham put down the file. "How do you mean?"

Laura's shoulders sank. "Well... But... It's just that... Well..."

"Miss Beecham, Laura," Graham began, "if I told you the top five most embarrassing things that have happened whilst I've been working here, you wouldn't believe three of them."

Laura couldn't help but laugh at that. She looked a little chilly, dressed only in a blouse and a long wrap skirt. "Well, alright then, I've locked myself out of the library."

Graham couldn't repress a chuckle. "I wondered if that might be it," he said. "Well, at least it's an easy fix." He tapped out a number from memory, spoke briefly with someone called Jock, and replaced the receiver. "Help is on its way. Now, if you don't mind me asking, how did you manage it?"

Laura began to relax a little. "I was putting some books in my car and the door shut behind me just after I'd set it to lock. The library keys are inside."

"You didn't call the other librarian for help?"

There was an embarrassed glance down to the lobby's linoleum floor. "I left my phone on the distribution desk. And, did you know, the police station is actually closer to the library than the nearest phone box?"

"I'm a bit surprised we still have any," Graham said. "But I'm pleased you came here first. The ever-helpful Jock will be along presently."

Laura raised an eyebrow. "Does he work for you?"

"No!" Graham laughed. "Jock is a very fine locksmith. He used to work for the wrong team, but these days, I put a little work his way when I can. Please, take a seat."

They waited together, sitting in the reception area's blue plastic chairs. "I haven't seen you around the White House Inn for a few days," Graham said.

"My shifts at the library mean that I grab a late breakfast and I miss dinner. Mrs. Taylor leaves a plate out for me. She said you'd been here about six months," Laura added, crossing her legs and rubbing her shoulders with both hands to warm up. "Down from London too, I hear?"

Graham grabbed his own jacket from the coat stand and offered it to Laura. "Ah, the formidable intelligence-gathering apparatus that is Mrs. Taylor," he marvelled. "Yes, I was in the Met, but I fancied a new start. Sounds like you're a little bit the same."

"Something like that," Laura said, gratefully sliding the jacket over her chilly shoulders. "London was getting a little too... how shall I say... *intense* for me. Too crowded, too big."

"Lots of people down here would agree," Graham said. "Jersey's a great escape from city life. It's quiet."

"So," Laura wondered, "you haven't been up to your ears in big cases?"

Graham gave an equivocating shrug. "Not up to my ears exactly, but there's been more action than I expected."

"Really?" Laura frowned.

"But most of it's small, everyday stuff that you see in police stations the world over. The odd drunk, theft, locked-out person…" His eyes twinkled as he looked over at Laura. She blushed and shrugged her shoulders.

"Mrs. Taylor mentioned that you helped out with something important right after you arrived. She was a bit cagey about what."

"I'm not surprised," Graham told her. "There was a poisoning there."

Laura blinked. "Really? But you caught the person responsible?"

Graham nodded. "It involved a little more drama than I'd have preferred, but yes."

"Congratulations," she said. "And I'm told that wasn't your only success."

The DI shrugged this off. "Our job is to catch criminals, Miss Beecham, Laura. Sometimes it takes longer than we'd like, even a few years," Graham said, remembering the long-delayed conclusion to the Beth Ridley case last November, "but we always try to get there in the end."

Laura looked at him curiously, a slight smile on her face. She wasn't quite sure what to make of him. He seemed accomplished but self-effacing, certainly reserved and something of a local hero by all accounts. There was a worldliness gained through his own undoubted competence that Laura found absorbing, especially on an evening when she was feeling particularly naïve and clueless. And lastly, a hint of melancholy presented itself, the source of which she suspected he kept very close to his chest.

"Ah, Jock," she heard him say. Graham rose to greet the locksmith, a stocky sixty-year old with more wrinkles on his weather-beaten face than there were hairs on his gleaming head. "I wonder if you're able to take things from here?" he asked Laura. "I gave the desk constable the night off so he could play for the Jersey Police five-a-side, and I don't want to leave the desk unmanned."

"No problem," Laura smiled. "You've been very helpful."

"My pleasure. And thanks, Jock," he said to the locksmith.

"Any time, guv'," the man said, snapping out a salute. "Come on then, m'lady. Let's get you fixed up."

"Please drop into the library if you're passing, Detective Inspector." Laura gave him one of her lovely smiles and followed Jock out to his van.

Graham watched them leave and returned to his seat behind the reception desk. Eventually, he opened his file and started reading again. First, however, he stared out of the window into the Gorey night, deep in thought. He picked up his pen and made a list of all the points of local history he had been meaning to research since he'd arrived on Jersey but hadn't yet. Surely, he thought, it was high time he did.

Nobby found that the best method of staying awake was to patrol the museum's rooms in a random pattern, and keep adjusting the lighting. He ambled from the grand entrance, past the ticket desk, and into the ballroom, ensuring once more that the windows were all locked and that everything was in its place. He shone his torch around the dark room, under the piano and along the rows of paintings on the walls. "Right as rain," he said. This was another of his habits. Nobby was fond of chattering away to himself to help pass the time.

The three-room display suite at the back, once a

drawing room, library, and smoking lounge, was also in good order. He had long since become familiar with their illustrious bequest. The desk's mother-of-pearl inlay shone, iridescent, in his flashlight's glow. "Ezekiel Satterthwaite," he tried. "Now there's a name to conjure with."

The night guard position was proving the ideal way for Nobby to earn a little extra money to supplement his government pension. It helped him to afford the occasional Saturday afternoon down the pub, preferably one with a big screen that was showing premiership football. He liked to work steadily through three or four pints whilst enjoying a well-played game. Nobby returned to the ballroom and sat on the bench of the grand piano for a moment's rest when he heard the unmistakable sound of glass breaking.

"Oi!" he hollered. He rose quickly, a little too quickly. His head swam. He trotted toward the source of the sound. It had come from the museum's rear. "Is someone there?" he called. He turned on the lights and looked left toward the mannequins and then right. There was a large man dressed all in black, his face masked by a scarf standing next to the Satterthwaite desk. The man was frozen in the beam of Nobby's torch.

"Alright, just hold it there. Let's not have any trouble," Nobby began, more calmly than he felt. He wasn't armed, but he knew the torch could do some damage if it were wielded with force. He also had a radio tuned to the police frequency.

"Don't move," the man said. He had a very deep, gruff voice. "I said, *don't move*." Nobby saw now that there was a revolver in the intruder's hand, a snub little .38.

The night watchman's hand stopped short of his radio's buttons. "Take it easy, mate," he breathed, his heart thumping loudly in his ears. "No need for anyone to get hurt." Nobby felt a pain in his chest.

"Hands on your head," the man said, his voice low and brusque.

The intruder's demeanour, his clothes, the gun, small but powerful and useful at close range, all told Nobby he was facing a seasoned professional. He knew he should do as he was told, but Nobby hated being pushed around, and the museum at night was *his* responsibility.

"What kind of silly bugger breaks into a little, local *museum*?" Nobby asked. "They'll have you for armed robbery, so they will. Ten years, that'll cost you, if not more."

The figure in front of him was not in the least intimidated. The gun rose slightly. "What would *murder* cost me?" he growled.

CHAPTER ELEVEN

THE RED PHONE rang just as Jim Roach was setting his morning coffee down on the desk. "Gorey Police," he said and then listened. He made quick notes on the pad of white forms kept by the phone. "Understood," he said. "Ambulance on its way?" "Good. Ten minutes. Remind the crew to tread carefully," he said.

Graham had heard the phone and was at his office door reaching for his jacket. "Constable?"

"Body discovered at the museum, sir. Curator called it in." Roach began to phone Sergeant Harding, whose shift wasn't due to start for another six hours. He was following the procedure Graham had drummed into them in the event of a major incident. After that, he'd call Barnwell.

"Damn," Graham observed momentarily, but then he straightened up. "Right, I'll be on my way. See you there." He donned his jacket and headed to the museum alone, knowing that Roach would catch up.

On the way, Graham called Tomlinson. "Marcus, body at the museum."

"Just got the call, old chap. I'll be right there as soon as I finish my breakfast." Graham imagined the pathologist sitting at his dining table, boiled egg in its cup, meticulously set aside buttered toast, a glass of freshly squeezed orange juice and equally freshly brewed coffee. He hoped Tomlinson wouldn't be too long about it. "First thing on a Monday morning, eh?" Graham marvelled as he steered his marked police car speedily along the lanes which linked Gorey to the rest of the island.

"Death always comes at a bad time," Tomlinson said, deadpan. "I'll be there soon. Tell the ambulance crew not to..."

"I know, Marcus."

The ambulance was already parked at the entrance to the museum when Graham got there. The detective inspector walked around it to find a short, balding man leaning against the outside wall of the building. He was shaking tiny green mints from a small plastic container into the palm of his hand.

"Sorry," he said nervously, tossing a couple of the mints into his mouth and obliterating them immediately with a decisive crunch. "I'm not dealing with this very well."

"Who are you, sir?" Graham asked.

"Sorry," the man said again, wiping his palms on his suit jacket. "Adam Harris-Watts. I'm the curator of the museum."

"Good morning, sir," Graham said with a more sympathetic tone. "You were the one who found the body, I understand?"

"Yes," Harris-Watts said, his jaw twitching for another mint to grind. "It was awful. I mean, I've known Nobby for three years. Such a nice fellow..." The curator sniffed.

"We'll find out what happened here," Graham

promised. "There's nothing you could have done." He had said the very same things for over a decade to bereaved spouses, parents, siblings, and other loved ones who were out of their minds with grief. "When my colleague, Constable Roach arrives, he'll take a statement from you. Then you'll be free to spend the rest of the day as you wish."

Harris-Watts coughed. "I have to call the museum's board right now. They'll need to know what's happened."

"Alright, just please don't go anywhere," Graham said. He left the agitated man and walked past the ticket desk and into the ballroom where he spotted the paramedics standing in a room at the back of the house. It was filled with paintings and artefacts, as well as a strikingly beautiful desk. At its feet lay the body of a man in a blue sweater and black trousers. His first thought was that there was less blood than he'd expected.

"Morning Sue, Alan," he said to the ambulance crew.

Sue Armitage and Alan Pritchard were dressed in blue overalls, but were standing away from the body. "Morning, DI Graham. Great way to start a Monday, eh?"

"What have we got?" Graham asked, his hand reflexively bringing out his notepad and pencil.

"Night watchman. No signs of a pulse when we arrived. Seems like he's been dead for a few hours, at least. Thought it best to leave him until you got here," Sue said.

Marcus Tomlinson bustled into the room, carrying his black leather bag and a large travel mug of coffee. "Has he been moved?" the veteran pathologist asked at once.

"No, Marcus. Sue and Alan know your drill, just like I do," Graham reassured him.

"Good," Marcus said. "Good. Well done." Tomlinson visibly relaxed, took a swig of coffee, and handed the mug to

Graham. "Hold onto this for me." The pathologist set down his bag and approached the body, immediately beginning to dictate his findings into his mobile phone. Graham looked around but, unable to find a suitable place to set Tomlinson's coffee, held onto it. The two paramedics exchanged a glance. They were required to stay until the body could be moved, and so were able to watch the highly experienced—even *famous*, at least in a local sense—Marcus Tomlinson at work.

"The deceased has been preliminarily identified as Charles Norris, known to everyone as 'Nobby'," the pathologist was saying. "Formal identification will take place before the post-mortem. The body is lying face down, at the foot of the Satterthwaite desk, his head almost touching the right front leg of the desk. His left arm is splayed out under the desk itself." At the pathologist's request, Graham handed him the camera from his black bag, ultimately deciding to set Tomlinson's coffee on the floor next to it. The pathologist began taking close-up photographs. "The head is turned slightly to the right, and there's a quantity of blood underneath it. There's an obvious laceration to the left temple." Tomlinson looked more closely. "A cranial avulsion. There's also damage to the near-right corner of the desk, indicating that he fell and struck his head on it."

Graham peered closely. He winced at the obvious marring of the desk's workmanship, especially in such a manner. A smear of Nobby's blood was visible on the cracked wood. "Are you thinking it was an accident?" he asked during a lull in Tomlinson's recording.

"I'm thinking," the pathologist retorted, "that it was a fall. But that's all we can say, as yet."

Graham knew that Tomlinson was, above all, a scientist. He would never jump to a conclusion. For the pathologist, evidence was the sole arbiter of events. Nothing beyond it would be considered, especially at such an early stage.

"Alright, I'm going to take some measurements," Tomlinson announced. "DI Graham, this won't be very pleasant, I'm afraid." The examiner lifted Nobby's blue sweater and white shirt a few inches up his back and asked for Graham to bring his bag.

"He has to measure the temperature," Sue whispered knowingly to Alan. Sue had had five years with the States of Jersey Ambulance Service. She was fascinated by forensic pathology and liked to read up on the subject in her spare time, preferably in a sunny room accompanied by a mug of tea and her bulldog, Chester, snoring by her side. "But we can't just use the surface of the skin or inside the mouth because we need to take the *core* temperature," she explained to him. "Dr. Tomlinson will take a reading from within an internal organ. Typically," she added, "the liver." Alan listened patiently. He'd only been with the ambulance service for two years. He was Sue's junior, a fact she repeatedly reminded him of one way or another.

Tomlinson made an incision and gained his reading. "So, you're a budding pathologist, eh?" he said, managing a friendly smile as he stood once more and turned to Sue.

"Thinking about taking some courses, sir, yes." Sue was petite, about twenty-six with dark hair tied back in a short ponytail.

"Then you might be able to tell me how long ago this poor man died. Fancy giving it a try?"

She nodded. "What's his core temperature now, sir?"

"Eighty-nine point eight degrees Fahrenheit," Tomlinson announced. "Or thirty-two point one degrees Celsius, for the metrically minded. What does that tell you?"

Sue did the maths in her head. "That the victim has lost just under nine degrees Fahrenheit since death," she said. "Typically, corpses lose one-point-five degrees per hour, so we can say he died around six hours ago." She checked her watch. "Two in the morning."

"Excellent. Now, let's see if the remaining evidence confirms that hypothesis. Let's turn him." The two paramedics and Tomlinson gingerly tipped Nobby's body to the right and then laid him out flat on his back. They lifted his sweater and unbuttoned his shirt. "You see this, DI Graham?" Tomlinson asked.

Graham was examining the paintings and other objects in the room. He turned quickly and immediately recognised the purple-blue marks on the victim's chest and abdomen. "Lividity," he said.

"The pooling of blood under gravity, after the heart stops beating," Tomlinson confirmed, turning to Sue and continuing his quiz. "But is it *fixed* or not?"

Graham watched Tomlinson tutor the two much younger medics in the basics of forensic pathology for a moment and then turned back to the paintings. It was so like Marcus to make these opportunities, 'teachable moments,' a chance to impart a little knowledge and help the next generation gain some practical experience.

"It's not quite fixed," Sue decided. "Once we turned him onto his side, the purple patches began to move slowly away from his abdomen and toward his ribs."

"A very significant conclusion," Tomlinson said, impressed. "Because fixed lividity begins at around eight to twelve hours after death, and we can therefore state…?" he said.

"That the six-hour estimate of time elapsed since death is still roughly correct," Sue said.

"Or, more specifically, that the poor man expired no more than eight hours ago, and probably between six and eight," Tomlinson told them. "So, what does that tell us about the time of death?"

"Between midnight and two?" Alan dared.

"Spot on. Now, one more thing to examine before we move the body to the lab. Anyone want to guess what it is?" Graham remained silent, perusing the collection and allowing Tomlinson his professorial moment. Neither Alan nor Sue responded. "Rigor mortis," Tomlinson said with a flourish. "Take his fingers... go on," he said to the reluctant Sue. "Can you move them?"

"A little bit," Sue said, taking the pale fingers in her gloved hands with obvious distaste.

"But the grip is not yet *rigid*, you'd say?"

"Not yet," she agreed.

CHAPTER TWELVE

ROACH APPEARED JUST as the three medics were pressing and turning the dead man's joints. He shivered at the sight. "I've been looking around the outside of the building, and I've found something, sir. In the store room on the other side of the house," he whispered to Graham, not wanting to disturb the others.

"Right, good lad," Graham whispered back. "I'll be along in five."

Tomlinson checked Nobby's elbows and knees. "A little more than halfway to complete stiffness, I'd wager," he said. "This tells us *two* things. It's more evidence for our time-of-death hypothesis, because rigor sets in completely within twelve hours. But if we're right, and his death occurred between midnight and two o'clock, his state of rigor mortis should be much more pronounced than it is. Our victim must have had a high level of ATP in his system when he died."

"ATP?" Alan asked. He was younger than Sue, perhaps early twenties, and had bright, curious eyes that darted around, gathering data quickly as they went. The two paramedics were the opposite of the cynical, jaded, older types Graham had experienced in London.

"Adenosine triphosphate," the inspector told them from the other side of the room, where he was examining a case of military medals. "It's a chemical which is important for muscular energy. ATP is sustained by oxygen from our blood flow, but that obviously ceases at death. This loss of ATP brings about the muscular stiffness we call rigor mortis."

"Excellent, DI Graham. If you weren't such a fine detective, I'd recommend switching careers to medicine," Tomlinson said. "So, we're able to conclude that our victim died somewhere between midnight and two o'clock. He fell onto his front and wasn't moved. He definitely hit his head on this desk, causing a serious wound to his left temple. But was that what *killed* him?" Tomlinson asked.

His younger companions looked at him, wide-eyed. "We'll find out later when we get him back to the morgue," Tomlinson finished disappointingly. He directed the paramedics to wrap the body in plastic. He then watched as they carefully transferred it to a black body bag and onto the waiting gurney. Tomlinson walked out with them to the ambulance. Graham followed.

"What's your gut telling you, Marcus?" he asked. "Natural causes, or...?"

"He fell," the older man repeated. "I'll know more by the end of the day."

Graham frowned. "I've got a funny feeling about this one," he said as the ambulance doors closed. "Let me know as soon as you have anything."

Tomlinson shook the DI's hand. "Depend on it."

Turning away, Graham saw that standing outside the

front entrance watching the ambulance trundle off down the street was the museum curator.

"Mr. Harris-Watts?" Graham said as the vehicle disappeared from view. The man, despite his earlier distress, seemed reluctant to drag his eyes away from the sight to focus on Graham.

"Yes?"

Graham ushered him inside. "We need to have a further word, sir. Would you be so kind as to walk me through your collections?"

It had not taken Constable Roach long to find the broken window at the back of the museum. It opened onto a storeroom for objects that were 'resting.' They were items that were either part of the museum's rotating displays or were awaiting repair or appraisal.

"The intruder," Roach concluded, "broke this window, climbed through into the museum, and then left the same way."

"Damn," Harris-Watts said bitterly. "The blighter did something as *simple* as break in through a window?"

"We'll see." Graham looked around the room. "Tell me more about the method of entry, Roach. What does it show us?"

"He just broke the glass and climbed through, sir," Roach said. "There's no obvious attempt to force the window open, or to saw, or cut around the lock. Guess he wanted to just get in, do his business, and get out. What did Dr. Tomlinson say about our victim?"

"Just that he fell. I think he had a heart attack *before* he fell or died from a head wound *when* he fell." Harris-Watts shuddered.

Roach lifted his eyebrows as high as they would go. "Dr. Tomlinson wouldn't like us speculating about Mr. Norris's death, sir. Not without any evidence."

"That's true. So, let's not tell him, eh?" Graham quietly ushered Roach between the shelves of stored artefacts and back into the room that housed the Satterthwaite desk. He turned back. "Please come with us, Mr. Harris-Watts." Turning to Roach once more he said, "There's glass everywhere. See how some of it has been ground into the wood?"

Roach knelt and examined the crushed glass. "It's almost powdered, sir."

"So?" Graham posed. "That tells us something more, doesn't it?"

Roach thought quickly. "That he collected glass on his clothes on his way through the window?" He looked back in the direction of the intruder's entry point. "That the intruder was a big lad?" he surmised,

"A man in all likelihood," Graham agreed. "And not a slight one. What else do we have?"

Roach swiped his iPad. "Well, Mr. Harris-Watts here," Roach looked up to acknowledge the curator, "told me earlier that the CCTV footage is nearly useless, because the victim kept most of the lights off."

"Blast," Graham swore. "They weren't night-vision cameras?"

Harris-Watts shook his head. "Too costly," he explained.

"What about footage of Nobby's death?"

The curator was red-faced now. "The frame rate is so low that... Well, Constable, you've seen it..."

"In one frame, he's standing up," Roach explained, "and in the next, he's on the floor."

Graham's temper frayed. "Bloody hell." He stopped himself from saying more.

"I'm sorry, it's the budget, and..." Harris-Watts appeared to be trembling. He shakily tapped out two more mints into his palm and threw them into his mouth.

Graham had his hands aloft. "I get it. But that doesn't mean it's not frustrating. Corner shops have better security." Thoroughly chastised, Harris-Watts appeared to be approaching tearfulness. Graham calmed himself and gave the curator a conciliatory look. "Alright. I suppose it can't be helped now. But make sure you speak to us later. We'll advise you on appropriate security measures for items of this value in future."

"Mr. Harris-Watts also stated that there's nothing missing from the museum," Roach reported, looking for a way to move on from the camera-related impasse.

"Not a thing, as far as I can see," the curator confirmed. "Perhaps the burglar changed his mind, or ran?"

DI Graham took a close look at Adam Harris-Watts for a moment. "Nothing whatsoever missing?"

The curator wriggled under the investigator's stern gaze. "No," he frowned awkwardly. "Why?"

Graham ignored his question. "I wonder if you'd be good enough to account for your whereabouts last night."

Harris-Watts gulped and took a step back. Roach watched him carefully. "I was... at home," Harris-Watts stammered. "You can't think..."

"Alone?" Graham asked.

"Yes," Harris-Watts said with a shrug.

"Very well. Captain J. R. D. Forsyth of the Royal Jersey Militia."

Harris-Watts stared at Graham again, none the wiser. "What about Captain Forsyth?"

"A recipient of numerous medals during the First World War, or so your display claims. Among them is the Military Medal, quite a high honour."

"Yes," the curator said. "Captain Forsyth is something of a local hero, celebrated for his bravery during the assault at—"

"It's missing."

Harris-Watts stared at him before dashing at once to the cabinet, a horrified expression on his face. "But..."

"Roach? I'll let you ask the obvious question," Graham said.

"Why carry out a risky, dangerous break-in, possibly a murder, enter a room full of valuable, portable objects," Roach wondered, "and then only steal a single medal from a large collection?"

"But these are priceless!" Harris-Watts was saying. "They're irreplaceable historical artefacts!"

Graham took Roach to one side, "Whatever happened here, whether it was a burglary or something else, it's certain that our victim died in the middle of it, and probably *because* of it, one way or another. So, what are our chief questions here, Constable?"

Roach straightened his back. "Who broke in? And, no matter what was taken, why did they take it?"

CHAPTER THIRTEEN

LILLIAN HART SAT in a deep purple armchair in her living room, watching her most important client very carefully. She took a long drag of her unfiltered cigarette, letting the smoke escape languidly from her mouth for a moment before she sucked it back in. Charlotte Hughes had just come to the end of a long and unexpected call, and she looked worryingly pale. "Is everything okay?"

Charlotte stared at her phone for a moment, and then typed something into it. "Hmm?"

"Was that important?" Lillian reframed, more honestly this time. She meant to keep tabs on her client. As Charlotte's Parliamentary campaign manager, Lillian had a strong aversion to Charlotte acting independently. That was how campaigns got out of control or fell behind in their constant battle to remain ahead of the news cycle and the swirling, unpredictable world of social media. It was imperative that Lillian knew everything. Nothing was to be acted upon unless it was run by her first.

"That was my brother, Eric. Something's happened on

Jersey. A museum's been broken into," Charlotte explained. She didn't look at Lillian as she set aside the phone.

"So?" Lillian asked, crossing her legs. "What's that got to do with the price of beef?"

"Oh, you know, the Channel Islands. My father's estate..." Charlotte trailed off. Her brow had knotted up during the call, and she tried to massage it and herself back into a more relaxed, unruffled state.

Lillian stared at her. "What are you blathering about? Do we need to take any action?" She asked the question in a tone that bluntly conveyed her desire to take exactly none. A plain woman, Lillian attempted to lift her large features by wearing garish make-up, an effort that mostly achieved the opposite of what she intended. Nevertheless, she was respected as an experienced and fearsome campaign manager with connections deep throughout the meandering web of British politics and the wider commerce, media, and national defence interests that supported it. She was not a woman to be trifled with.

Lillian was utterly focused on one thing and one thing only: getting Charlotte Hughes elected as a Member of Parliament. She had donated eighteen hours of her day, every day, for the last three months, as well as the use of her town house that was acting as campaign headquarters. Whatever this call was about, it seemed entirely unconnected to the matter at hand. It was therefore utterly irrelevant. Lillian expected Charlotte to put whatever this issue was aside and devote her energies to this evening's town hall meeting.

"No, no. Oh, I don't know. My father's desk is on display at a museum and—" Charlotte closed her eyes and shook her head.

Lillian was incredulous. "Desk?" She rolled her eyes.

She imagined some cheap, flat-pack affair assembled in half an hour amidst much cursing and temper. Charlotte went on to describe the Satterthwaite desk in great detail, but Lillian was hardly more impressed. "So, it's been stolen?" She was having a hard time following.

"Hardly," Charlotte responded dryly, stung by Lillian's dismissive tone. "It's been damaged."

Lillian sat up in her armchair. It was a measure of the dehumanising nature of professional politics that her first thought was to wonder whether this event could in any way harm Charlotte's bid for political office. She ran through a number of scenarios in her head, but after a few moments, she relaxed. The links were much too tenuous.

"I'm going to call our family lawyer," Charlotte said. "Give me a few minutes, and then we'll talk about tonight." Charlotte turned away to place the call.

Her campaign manager looked at her in bewilderment. "Go ahead, don't mind me." To Lillian, this was an entirely unwelcome interruption and an even more unnecessary one, but clearly it had to run its course before Charlotte could be free of it. The older woman stood and left just as the call went through, heading upstairs to powder her nose.

"Carl? It's Charlotte Hughes. Have you heard about the incident on Jersey?"

Forty minutes and several phone calls later, Lillian was beginning to lose her temper. This wasn't a surprise to anyone who knew her. Even when she wasn't dedicating herself wholeheartedly to a political campaign, she was known to fly off the handle at the least provocation. Why was Charlotte so bothered about her father's vintage office furniture? This *contretemps* in Jersey was materialising into what Lillian labelled 'a thing.'

"Look, I'm not going off the deep end," Charlotte protested. "Carl Prendergast told me that Don had asked about the desk not three days ago. And now there's been a break-in at the museum where it's on display. You have to admit it's a bit of a coincidence."

"What are you suggesting? That your stepbrother, for a reason we can't even guess, broke into a museum? Because of a *desk*?"

"I don't know. I don't know! It's just—"

"Why, in the name of *all* that is *holy*," Lillian said, struggling to keep her voice even, "might Don English, of all people, do that?"

"I have no idea. Don's a strange old boy," Charlotte admitted.

"I mean, it's just a *desk*, an inanimate object! You're overreacting." Lillian flapped her hand and looked away. Anger had a tendency to sharpen her already angular features, making her look both a few years older and as though she was wearing even more makeup than usual.

Charlotte held up her tablet to show Lillian a full-screen picture of the Satterthwaite desk in all its considerable glory.

"A very pretty desk, to be sure," Lillian conceded. "But, and I repeat, why would he *care*?" She frowned even harder and sat back in her armchair. "Hang on," she said. "Is this the same Don who had the batty mother?"

Charlotte sighed. "She died just recently."

Lillian groaned. "Your father had her committed to a loony bin!"

"She was very ill," Charlotte said pointedly. "She was a danger to herself. It was for her own good."

"Her own good. Yes. Only now we've got a potentially angry, bereaved, and possibly equally loony son with an axe to grind." Lillian swirled the ice cubes in the glass of gin she'd poured herself even though it was only eleven in the morning. She slugged back the dregs, her long, sharp, purple nails clacking against the glass.

"There's something else," Charlotte said, looking as though she hardly dare tell Lillian her next piece of news, like a child confessing she'd broken a window. "The night security guard hit his head on the desk. He died. They found his body this morning." Charlotte's eyebrows dropped over her darkened eyes.

"Oh, terrific." Lillian said, ever her combative, accusatory self. "So now, we've got a *murderous*, angry, recently bereaved stepson on the case. *Your* case, honey."

Charlotte stood and headed to the kitchen for some much needed water. Finding a glass in the cupboard, she said, "You're right, we're getting way, way ahead of ourselves. We're being neurotic. Don probably didn't have anything to do with this. We don't know whether the guard's death was murder, or an accident, or even natural causes." Lillian didn't seem to hear her. She had gone from thinking Charlotte was completely overdramatising the situation to making her own leaps of conjecture. Her thoughts about what Charlotte was suggesting and their prospects for her campaign were alarming. "We don't even know," Charlotte said, shouting over the running tap, "if Don was anywhere near the place. For all we know, he was tucked up in bed in some horrible little flat when it happened, in... where does he live again? Oh yes, Goslingdale." The two women shuddered in unison.

"Only he called Prendergast about the desk completely out of the blue, less than seventy-two hours ago," Lillian pointed out. They had switched roles now. "And he's been furious with your father for decades and, by extension, with you."

Coming back in the room, Charlotte sat and hooked her mousy brown hair behind her ears. She drank most of the glass of water. "No need for the extension," she said thinly. "We always hated each other. He was an annoying little blighter, and his mother... Well, I shouldn't speak ill of the dead," she said.

"Oh, don't stop now, Missy. You have to tell me *everything*," Lillian implored. "It's the only way I can protect you."

"We, Eric and I, always considered Susannah a gold-digger who tricked Dad into marrying her. He bent over backwards," Charlotte maintained, "to keep her happy. It wasn't his fault, or mine, that she went off the deep end. But Don seemed to think it was."

Lillian raised an eyebrow. She harboured few charitable illusions as to her client's family. Don's resentment toward the Hughes' was probably both deeply felt and legitimate. If Don was involved in this incident, this was, most definitely, going to be 'a thing.'

"But... why the *desk*? What would he want with it?" she asked. Charlotte finished her water. She was tapping her glass against her knee.

"Are you sure that's all this is, Charlotte?" Lillian leant forward, her elbows on her knees. She looked her client directly in the eyes. "Some crazy half-breed relative looking to take out his righteousness on a piece of old furniture?"

The younger woman sighed. Lillian, for once, waited. "There... there were rumours."

"About what?" Lillian pounced. Charlotte looked away.

"Charlotte..." Lillian remonstrated. "You need to tell me everything," she repeated.

"Rumours have swirled in my family for years that a letter exists that would shame us, possibly ruin us. We've never found any sign of it, but there was talk that Susannah was privy to the contents." Charlotte's voice was almost a squeak. "That might have been the reason my father put her in a mental institution." She looked away.

"Good grief, are you telling me that your father effectively incarcerated your stepmother for decades, smearing her name in the process, because she knew about some dodgy dealings of his?" Charlotte's head dipped minutely. Lillian stared at the wall, her foot jiggling furiously. "But I still don't see what it has to do with this blasted desk."

"After his death, Eric and I searched and searched. There was a rumour—"

"Rumours, again," Lillian spat, rolling her eyes.

Charlotte ignored her and continued in a small voice, "We thought that the desk might contain a secret compartment and the letter was in there. We looked for days. We even hired an expert. Eventually, we had to conclude that one didn't exist. Now I'm wondering if we were wrong. Maybe Susannah said something on her deathbed. Maybe she knew something I don't. And now maybe Don does."

Lillian threw her head against her chair back. "Whoa, this is bad. *Bad*." Throughout this discussion, Lillian had never stopped calculating.

"Okay," she said after a moment's thought. "We need to stop this before it starts. Here's what we're going to do. We need to find Don English. We need to keep the incident out of the national press, and you're not going to comment on it to anyone."

Charlotte squinted at Lillian. "Are you sure?" she asked.

Lillian waved away Charlotte's uncertainty. "I don't want your name anywhere near this," she said. "It's got nothing to do with you. We need to bury the story and do so immediately. What's happening with the desk?"

Charlotte glanced down at her notes. "Carl said Dad's estate will pay for the repairs. They'll cost a small fortune, but the museum will be hard-pressed to afford them otherwise. He's going to ask a local cabinetmaker to take a look at it."

"Good," Lillian said. "The sooner the better. Hopefully, it will all blow over. Keep your distance and stick to your schedule for the week. I don't want the media sniffing around."

But Charlotte already knew that was impossible. "Lilly, look. I know how important it is to keep our eyes on the prize, but you said yourself, we need to find Don."

"Let me deal with Don English," Lillian retorted.

"No, I'll go down there. I'll find out if it was him, if he was involved in this."

The campaign manager stared at her client as though Charlotte was proposing that she star in a Lady Godiva reenactment. "You'll do no such thing."

"Look," Charlotte said again.

"I'm not looking. I refuse to look."

"It'll only be for a few days," Charlotte argued.

"That's not the point! You need to stay here, canvassing, going door-to-door, holding town halls. You need to be seen doing the kinds of things that prospective Members of Parliament do to get elected. And you need to stay out of the tabloids. You do not want," Lillian insisted, "to get mixed up in a possible murder inquiry, with a mutinous stepbrother, or scandalous family revelations. Let me handle him."

"I have..." Charlotte began.

"Charlotte listen, I'm here," Lillian reiterated, "to help get you elected. And to protect you from scandal. This Jersey business has all the makings of a three-ringed circus, and you're going to back away from it with dignity and poise. You know, the kind of characteristics one associates with a professional and successful politician?"

Charlotte stood. "No."

Lillian stood too. This was *her* reputation, *her* time, *her* house. "If you go down there, I can't guarantee anything. If this incident had taken place in your constituency, I'd have you reading the eulogy at the guard's funeral. But no one *cares* about Jersey. It may as well be in the Cambodian jungle. Your place is *here*, winning votes among *these* people," she said, gesticulating wildly at the window.

But Charlotte was resolved. "Cancel tonight's town hall. Make up an excuse." She grabbed her tablet. "I'm booking a flight to Jersey."

CHAPTER FOURTEEN

THE PROUDEST MOMENT of Felipe Barrios' life had been back in 1998 when his friend and mentor erected a new sign above the door of their workshop, *Steadman & Barrios*. For the first time, Felipe saw his name alongside that of the finest craftsman he had ever known, and the two officially became partners in a successful and respected local business. Felipe had, as a newspaper profile expressed it at the time, "come an awfully long way."

The second proudest moment was being asked to carry out repairs to the Satterthwaite desk. Newly delivered and standing on the hastily cleared floor of his workshop, the desk was as significant to a professional cabinetmaker as Michelangelo's *David* was to a sculptor or as a Mozart concerto was to a musician. It was a model of artistic perfection. Even before beginning the initial assessment, Felipe stood for nearly an hour, freshly prepared coffee in hand, simply admiring the craftsmanship, the proportions, and the original wood tone. Some men fall in love with sports cars or sailboats. Felipe was in love with antique furniture, and none was more deserving of his affection and respect than the work of Ezekiel Satterthwaite.

All that marred the moment was the necessity of the repair. There were traces of blood on the battered front right edge of its surface. These would need to be scrupulously cleaned and disinfected, in case any bacteria might take up residence in the wood and spread their corrosive influence. Then the repairs could take place. Felipe confirmed that the wood hadn't been *ruptured* as much as *compacted* by the impact of the security guard's skull. This meant, thankfully, that he wouldn't need to source appropriate wood to replace any missing fragments. It would have been a near-impossible task. Instead, carefully chosen polish would raise the compressed area, and layer after painstaking layer, he would fill the compaction and return the spoiled corner to its former glory.

Felipe's wife, Rosa, came into the room. "How is it, my dear?" They spoke in Spanish. She knew to announce herself very quietly, lest she disturb her husband during a sensitive moment. "Will it take long?"

He looked at her fondly. Although they had been married for over forty years, his wife, with whom he'd been through so much, was to him still as beautiful as when they'd first met on the beach as teenagers. "Several weeks," he estimated. "These things cannot be rushed." Indeed, patience was a chief virtue in this kind of work, especially when a mistake could prove difficult or impossible to rectify.

Felipe's partner, Ernest Steadman had taught him that every step had to be carefully planned out. Planning detailed schema was just one of the skills he had learnt from his benefactor. The old man had been like a second father to the younger Felipe, and not once since Steadman's death five years before had he been absent from Felipe's nightly prayers.

"God will work through your hands, my love," Rosa said, placing her hand on Felipe's arm. He nodded and she quietly left him to work. He stood before the glorious Satterthwaite desk, reflecting upon the events that had brought him to this moment. Were it not for the most unlikely of incidents, neither his journey to Jersey, nor any of the memorable experiences he had enjoyed on the island since, would have materialised.

Two hours later, Felipe sat by the desk and examined the damage once more. "Such a shame," he muttered. He started removing the blood from the damaged area, using a non-acidic cotton swab soaked initially only in water. It was slow, painstaking work. He reached down to steady the desk against his gentle swabbing, his fingers finding the underside of the main drawer where it met the front brace of the desk. He felt a tiny depression in the wood.

Felipe stopped and put the swab aside, kneeling and then lying down to peer under the desk. His fingertips hadn't deceived him. There was a slight undulation. When he ran his fingers over it again, it felt manmade, deliberate, not the result of natural warping over the centuries. He pressed his fingertip into the indentation, and the desk resounded with a deep, metallic *thunk*.

Felipe started and stood fretfully, watching for any movement, terrified that he had broken a priceless masterpiece. Part of him feared that the desk, absent now some vital structural linchpin might simply fall into pieces on his workshop floor. But the desk was silent, and Felipe carefully approached once more.

His heart beat with excitement as he examined the underside of the desk. He suspected the slight indentation was a catch that opened a lock of some kind within it. He searched using his torch but found nothing in the side drawers or under the main body of the desk. When he pulled out the central drawer, however, it slid right to its limit and exposed a raised area at the back.

"Ezekiel, you crafty old..." Felipe had triggered an ingenious, lightweight mechanism unlike any he had ever seen. It had revealed a compartment hardly deeper than a deck of cards and almost as wide as the drawer itself. He stood and marvelled at his find. The existence of the compartment was hidden from anyone who was unaware of it. Certainly, the contents inside were not meant to be discovered casually. Felipe donned a new pair of surgical gloves.

Seconds later, he was on his knees, on the floor of his workshop. Stricken and immobile, all he was able to say, again and again, was, "*Madre de Dios....*"

CHAPTER FIFTEEN

AS SOON AS Charlotte turned her phone back on, seconds after her flight landed, it buzzed and beeped with a dozen messages. She ignored all but one. She knew without looking that most of them would be from Lillian, either begging her to return, or demanding an update. The only voicemail to which she listened was from Carl Prendergast.

"Charlotte, hi. Fantastic. I hope the two of you can let bygones be bygones. Here's Don English's number..." Perfect. Prendergast's never was the most incisive of legal minds.

Charlotte had only a cabin bag and was soon in a taxi on her way to a hotel in St. Helier. Her first order of business was to find out if Don really was on Jersey and figure out just what on earth was going on.

She dialled Don's number.

"Don English."

Don sounded as though she'd woken him up, and she wondered at once if he was suffering from another hangover. He always had drunk to excess.

"Don! It's Charlotte Hughes."

"Charlotte?" Don struggled to sit up in bed. Overnight the feathers in his pillow had migrated to opposite ends of the pillowcase, neither of which were now under his head. His camberwick bedspread lay on the floor.

"Charlotte," he repeated. Her features came to mind. She had a thin face with a pointed chin. Years ago, she'd had a long aquiline nose. Surgery had softened that feature, but Don still recalled the Wicked Witch of the West when he thought of her. At least she wasn't green.

"What are you doing calling me?" he asked.

"Carl gave me your number. I hope you don't mind. He told me about your Mother, Don. I'm so sorry. How are you doing?"

"I'm okay," he said warily. He rubbed sleep from his eyes and ran a hand over his rough chin. "How can I help you, Charlotte?" Don was immediately suspicious of this bolt from the blue. Charlotte and he hadn't spoken in years. He was quite sure she didn't give a hoot about his mother.

"I'm on Jersey..."

"You're on Jersey, too?" he said. Don was so surprised, the words slipped out before they'd registered in his brain.

"Why, yes. Are you? That's wonderful! Let's meet. It will be good to see you after all these years."

Don knew patently that this was a lie. The fog of sleep was lifting quickly now. Charlotte no more wanted to see him than he wanted to see her.

"Er, but what are you down here for?"

"There's been a incident at the museum involving the Satterthwaite desk. Do you remember? Dad's desk. I'm here to arrange for the repairs and show my face. Do the necessaries." Charlotte sounded positively chipper. "I know we haven't always been the best of friends but," she remembered Carl Prendergast's words, "can't we let bygones be bygones?"

She paused. When there was no response from Don, she pressed on. "Let's just talk. Meet me at the lookout point at Orgueil Castle. Would three o'clock work for you?"

There was a very long silence as Don seemed to weigh up the dangers of meeting his estranged, unpleasant, and potentially very powerful stepsister. "Alright. Three o'clock," he replied.

"Great. See you then. Byeee."

The meeting with Don arranged, Charlotte turned her attention to her other business in Gorey. Hopping once more into a taxi, she called and arranged to meet Adam Harris-Watts at the museum. Charlotte kept the meeting deliberately brief.

"I want to confirm that the Hughes estate will fund the repairs to the desk," she told the still-shaken curator. This was no small sum.

"That's so terribly kind of you. The museum would have been hard pressed..." Adam Harris-Watts spoke deferentially. An insurance claim for the full amount would have brought an unsustainable spike in the small museum's monthly premiums.

"Is there anything else?"

"Well, Nobby's—Mr. Norris' family—have set up a foundation in his name. It will provide football coaching for talented local youngsters. Nobby, Mr. Norris, was a big football fan. Perhaps...?"

'Yes, of course." Charlotte pulled out her chequebook.

"You know," Harris-Watts said as he showed Charlotte

out, back through the museum's grand entrance, "things like this aren't supposed to happen in museums. Only in *The Da Vinci Code* or something like that. Did you know your father visited the museum once? And I was the one who suggested to him that... Well, that our museum would be an appropriate display space for the desk. If I hadn't been so insistent, none of this would ever have..." Harris-Watts hung his head.

Charlotte took his arm and gave him her most sympathetic look. "Mr. Harris-Watts, Adam, this isn't your fault. It's just terribly unfortunate. We've always been tremendously happy to know that the desk is situated here, in a place representative of its history. You've done a fine job with it." The curator nodded his appreciation although he didn't take his eyes off the floor.

Charlotte continued, "I wonder, did you ever find anything in the desk? I heard Satterthwaite was famous for installing secret drawers. It was a childhood game of ours to look for one, but we were never successful." She was fishing. Sir Thomas would no more allow his children to play with his desk than he would sit them on his knee to read them a book.

"You're right about Satterthwaite." Adam Harris-Watts was on surer ground now. He spoke confidently. "But we think he only designed a piece with a compartment for every ten or so he made. At least that we know of. He never let on whether one of his designs contained a hidden drawer or not. It was his little joke. And he only made three desks in his entire career. That's why this one is so valuable. I don't believe either of the others has a compartment. Not one that's been discovered, anyway. Certainly, I examined your father's desk many times but never found one."

"Hmm. So what do the police think about it all?"

Harris-Watts popped a tiny mint into his mouth, orange this time. "They're as baffled as we are but they're working on it," he said as he ground his jaws. "They seem to think it might have been just a plain old break-in. Nothing to do with the desk. They're not even sure if Nobby's death was connected at all. Either way, it's terrible."

"Yes, quite," Charlotte tilted her head sympathetically. "Do they have any idea who it might have been? Nothing on camera?" She looked up at the small grey device mounted discreetly above the entrance to the museum.

The curator shook his head. "Our old camera system is so awful that there are only a couple of blurry frames. The police did say that it must have been a heavyset man who broke in, though."

It was hardly a description that narrowed down the field, but it also fit one person in particular. "Well, I'm sure we both wish them success in their investigations. There's really no need to hold yourself responsible," she told him again. "You're no more to blame than Satterthwaite himself or my father for that matter. What's going to happen now?"

"The desk went for repair as soon as your father's estate so graciously offered to cover the costs. The speed with which the repairs are effected can make a big difference to their success in these cases." Harris-Watts smiled at Charlotte obsequiously. "Fortunately we have the ideal person on the island. Felipe Barrios. Your father's desk is in expert hands. Barrios has been a fine furniture maker for nearly forty years. He will know exactly what to do."

Charlotte gave the downcast curator an awkward hug. She was relieved to leave the company of this fragile, fawning man. Once she'd shrugged him off, she set off with purpose to the castle for what was her main business of the day.

"Marcus?" Graham said, clicking the button on his desk phone, "What's new?"

"I'm calling about Mr. Norris, the guard at the museum. I've got a cause of death for you."

Graham took a deep, deliberate breath. "Let me have it, Marcus."

"Massive heart attack. Clear as day. Untreated, he wouldn't have been long for this world, even without the shock of the situation he was in."

After blinking several times, Graham began re-visualising the scene. "Could he have been saved?"

"Anything is possible, but it's doubtful. His arteries were shocking."

"So he just keeled over? The intruder didn't push him or hit him with anything?"

"No signs of struggle, no DNA. Nothing to connect him with an attacker at all," Marcus replied. "For all we know, he could have died before the burglary took place."

"So it might be just a big coincidence?"

"Except I didn't think you believed in coincidences," the pathologist said.

Graham chewed his lip. "Thanks, Marcus. We'll add it to the mix."

"Sorry I can't be of more help."

Graham sighed and put his phone down. He looked at the CCTV footage in front of him. Roach was right. It was practically useless. He'd spent the last thirty minutes scouring the two frames that contained the security guard's last recorded moments. Graham's eyes bored into the images in front of him, willing some clue to make itself apparent.

"Tea, guv?" Janice poked her head around the door. She didn't like to make him tea. It was a bit like offering cheap plonk to a sommelier. She doubted her tea would stand up to his scrutiny, but she didn't feel she could leave him out if she was boiling the kettle.

"Hmm? Oh, no thanks." Graham sat back and blew out his cheeks. "Here, come and take a look at these. Can you see anything useful in them?"

Janice walked over to stand behind him. She leant over his shoulder, looking intently at the screen in front as Graham flicked back and forth between the two frames.

"There... And there," Janice said.

"What? What is it you're seeing—?" Graham peered at the screen, his chin jutting out as he concentrated.

Janice pointed at the first frame. "That shadow there. You can just see it, v-e-r-y faintly. Nobby turns toward it. And look, his hand holding the torch is raised just a smidge... There was definitely someone there, sir. And Nobby was alive when they were."

Graham squinted, seeing the scene in front of him anew. Now that Janice had pointed it out, he could see what was perfectly obvious. He turned his head slowly to look at his sergeant, who was grinning cheerfully. "Thank you, Harding. You've been very helpful," he said slowly.

"My pleasure, sir. Sure you don't want any tea?"

CHAPTER SIXTEEN

DON WAS SITTING in a small coffee shop finishing his second cup whilst reading through yet another webpage on his laptop. The call from Charlotte had come as a harsh, unwelcome surprise, but the longer he dwelled on it, the thought of meeting her became less worrying. This would be a strange and probably quite difficult reunion, but it might prove useful if he played his cards right.

Don rubbed his eyes. He'd been doing more research into his "project," as he'd begun to call it. His latest efforts were starting to bear fruit, and his three piles of documents had grown considerably. Using his ancient laptop and the coffee shop's frustratingly slow internet connection, he had pieced together what he knew and had begun searching for relevant terms.

Don had concluded that there was only one convincing answer as to the identity of Sir Thomas' friend—the man with whom he was pictured in the photo his mother had mentioned but whose friendship he had kept secret. Based on the clues his mother had given him, Don had come to believe that the man was none other than the president of San Marcos, the despised and reviled General Augusto Fuente.

Almost the definition of a "savage dictator," Fuente had been a young and ambitious army officer when he and his cohort of disaffected right-wing militarists overthrew the democratic government in the early 1970s. The results were terrible but predictable. The new *junta* took control of the media, employed heavy-handed secret police tactics, and were responsible for a depressing litany of "disappearances." Some fifteen percent of the population fled, among them anyone with money or an education. All of this left Fuente subject to sanctions and isolated by the UN. In response, Fuente courted black marketers, smugglers, and those with flexible morals. It was just possible, Don thought, that Sir Thomas Hughes had been among the General's new friends.

The idea made Don laugh at first. It sounded like something out of a spy novel. But he double-checked, and it was the only theory that fit all of the available facts. Fuente was an international pariah, and nobody in their right mind would have boasted of their close friendship with him. However, the General was also rich, something of a playboy, and certainly the kind of man to court wealthy foreign guests by inviting them onboard his yacht. The *Gypsy Princess*, Don was amazed to find, was still owned by the "first family" of San Marcos. It had even been recently photographed in an exclusive marina, only a stone's throw from the presidential palace.

As Don thought this through, he became convinced his theory was correct. He reasoned that, though he could not guess what it might reveal, the content of the letter he was searching for could be a huge embarrassment to his stepsister should it become known. As the time of their meeting approached, Don began to imagine what the letter might say. Perhaps it would reveal humiliating secrets or past indiscretions. Worse still—or *better* still, depending on one's point of view—it might even reveal past crimes. Any of these would be enough to derail Charlotte's bid to become a Member of Parliament.

Don sighed. Whilst she had never bullied him or his mother outright, neither had Charlotte ever stuck up for them against her father who had. The father-daughter bond had been fast. At times, he'd come upon them whispering together, stopping abruptly when he came in the room. He'd always suspected they were plotting against him. Or his mother.

Don found his rain jacket and prepared to set off toward the castle, wondering what the outcome of this rather clandestine meeting might be. Charlotte was now a public figure. Reputation was everything to her. But his, and certainly his mother's honour needed defending.

He looked at his watch. It was 2:50 PM. He was going to be late. He quickly shuffled his papers together, shoved his laptop in his bag, and hurried to the door. He pulled it open and rushed through it, immediately slamming hard into the solid wall of uniform that stood on the other side. Don's papers flew like confetti into the air.

"Careful there, mate," Barnwell said. It was time for the constable's regular afternoon croissant, and he was very much looking forward to it.

"Sorry, sorry," Don said, frantically dropping to the floor to pick up the splayed papers.

"Here, let me help you, sir," Barnwell offered.

"No need, no need," Don replied, shoving the papers haphazardly into the buff folder he was carrying.

"Okay, then," Barnwell said, standing up and squinting curiously at the harried man. He watched bemused as Don scurried up the street to his car. "It's amazing the effect I have on people," he murmured. He looked down at his feet and noticed under one of the outdoor tables, between the legs of two chairs, was propped a loose sheet of paper. Barnwell bent down and picked it from the floor. He cast a glance at the sheet in front of him.

"One decaf almond milk latte and a chocolate croissant!" yelled the woman behind the café counter so loudly that she could be heard through the café's glass door. She held a lidded cup and paper bag aloft.

Barnwell opened the door, rolling the paper up and sticking it in his back pocket. "Ah, thanks Ethel. You're a love. Just what I need."

CHAPTER SEVENTEEN

SIR THOMAS HAD been a National Trust member for fifty years, and Charlotte had run around the gardens and ballrooms of more stately homes and elegant, preserved townhouses than she could count. But this imposing medieval fortress was in a different class entirely. It was a manmade *mountain*, solid and huge and resolutely immobile, commanding the coastline as if defying anyone to trespass on its shores. As she paid her entrance fee and walked through the inner courtyards, Charlotte noted that its massive blocks of worn stone could have been hewed and placed there by giants. It was a place of fairy stories, of roaring ogres and witches on broomsticks, intrigue captured in every crevice.

And yet, standing on its slightly windy battlements up top, dressed in a shabby raincoat and faded jeans, an old, crumpled backpack hanging off his shoulder, was Don English.

"Bracing, isn't it?" she said as she emerged onto the broad walkway that encircled the castle.

He turned to see her approach, his face curiously impassive. "Looks like we've got the same taste in springtime holiday destinations," he said flatly.

As Charlotte had hoped, the battlements were quiet. They'd be able to talk without being disturbed. "It's been a while, Don. How are you?"

He stared out over the sea, which was a shifting, blue-white carpet on this March afternoon. "Mum's gone," he said simply.

"I'm so sorry, Don."

"That's what people say, isn't it?" Don remarked. "They *say* they're sorry."

Charlotte could see the weight of the emotional burden Don carried. It was there in his posture, in the way he dressed, in the tone of his voice. The sadness. The resentment. She searched for an appropriate response. "I hope there wasn't suffering."

Don chuckled humourlessly before drawing a breath, the air hissing between his crooked, yellow teeth, "You know *damn well* that she suffered. Too much, and for too many years." Don turned to look at his stepsister.

Charlotte put a hand, very carefully, on the upper arm of Don's jacket. "They're gone. My father, your mother. Now it's just us. Let's at least try to be friends for a little while."

Don gathered himself and wiped his face on the sleeve of his jacket. "Yeah... So, how's the *campaign* going?"

Charlotte blinked for a moment. "It's going well, I suppose. Still two months to go, but my campaign manager thinks we're on the right track."

"You know," Don said, glancing at his feet, "I saw a billboard with your face on it yesterday. Made me wonder what it would look like on TV, in Parliament chambers."

Charlotte smiled, though she doubted this was the

warm endorsement it seemed to be. "I hope we'll find out soon."

"It's a safe seat," Don pointed out. "A great way to get yourself shoehorned into the House of Commons."

Charlotte was as aware of her background as anyone. The daughter of a rich businessman, carefully selected by the party for her connections as well as her acumen, she would be open to allegations of cronyism and dodgy dealing, almost from the outset. "There's always someone," she told him, rather frostily, "who won't like what I do. But I want to serve the people of my constituency."

Don produced a wry grin. "I hardly think so," he finally managed. "I know you too well. And I know the family you come from."

Charlotte sighed and pushed hair out of her eyes. "Why are you here, Don? On Jersey?"

He regarded her coolly for a second. "I'm taking a break," he said. "Getting away from it all."

"Really? Right when the museum is broken into and Dad's desk is damaged? Something of a coincidence isn't it?" Charlotte waited for his reaction to this verbal grenade. Don remained silent, his jaw bunching rhythmically.

Charlotte came closer, their shoulders almost touching as they looked out to sea. She angled her face so he had to look at her. She looked deep into his eyes and spoke slowly. "Did you have anything to do with that, Don? The break-in?" she asked.

"Of course not." Don closed his eyes, his shoulders tense, his fists clenched. He pulsed with a burst of fury. "You've misjudged me, my whole life. My *whole* life." he said, his tone laced with accusation.

"Alright, Don, alright," Charlotte said, backing off. She didn't know him as a violent man, but he was strong and powerful, and clearly harboured a grudge. "You're upset. Don, look," she said, moving forward again and placing her hand gently, tentatively, on his forearm, "you'll feel better if you tell *someone* what happened. Why don't you tell me?"

Don turned away again, flexing his arm to dislodge her hand. "What are you talking about?"

"On Sunday night. Tell me. I don't want to believe you could hurt anyone, Don. Certainly not over something like this."

Now he turned to her, blinking, confused. "*Hurt* anyone?"

"The guard. The one who died," she said quietly, careful not to sound accusatory. "It was an accident, wasn't it?"

Don's mouth fell open. "*Died?*" he stuttered. "What?"

"What did you want with the desk, Don?" Charlotte persisted. "Why were you there?"

Don's hands were fixed, vice-like, on the stone wall of the fortress, as if he feared a strong gust of wind might blow him from the battlements and into the Channel.

"I don't know what you're talking about," he repeated. "I didn't hurt anyone. Do you really think I'd risk a criminal record, my life, all over your vile father's lump of old wood?

"Then why are you here? On Jersey?"

"It was something my mother said," he managed to utter through gritted teeth. "The day she died."

"What did your mother say about it?"

"She said your father was always sitting there. At the desk, working. I just wanted to see it for myself. Yes, I went to the museum to see it, but in *daylight*. I never laid a finger on any guard."

"So that's all this is, Don? A trip? A quest to satisfy your curiosity over something you've never professed to be interested in before and one I can't fathom why you'd be interested in now?"

She turned to leave, but Don caught her arm. "Off back to that quaint, oh-so twee constituency of yours? Market Ellestry isn't it?" he said sweetly, drawing breath. "More campaigning to do?"

Charlotte shrugged. "Actually, I thought I'd stay around here for a couple of days," she said, lifting her chin and looking down her nose at him. Her tone changed and her face became a dark scowl. "Enjoy your little *break*."

Charlotte wrestled her arm from Don's grip and stalked back to the doorway, the steps down to street level unfurling behind it. She left Don alone with the wind, the bright, sparkling ocean, and his own gnawing worries. It was time to take a different tack.

CHAPTER EIGHTEEN

GRAHAM BEGAN A third page of notes, flipping through another volume on eighteenth-century furniture until he found the section he needed. Amidst the peace and quiet of a space intended only for learning and research, he was dedicating an hour to understanding the *context* of the object in this case. It made a pleasant change from interviewing low-rent criminals and calming upset and irate members of the public. His general knowledge was broad. He could usually answer eight out of ten questions on *Mastermind*, even the specialist rounds, and on more than one occasion, he had found himself banned from Jersey pub quizzes after inordinate solo successes. Nevertheless, he was ignorant on the work of Ezekiel Satterthwaite.

The records showed that the desk by which Nobby had been found was one of only three Satterthwaite ever made. The others resided in the private study of Emperor Akihito of Japan and in the opulent Sultan's Palace in Brunei. At auction, a Satterthwaite desk would, according to one estimate, fetch at least $1 million and perhaps much more.

Graham tutted when he read this. Displaying an asset worth that much without investing in comprehensive security measures or even informing the local police of its value was negligent bordering on the criminal. No wonder Adam Harris-Watts was such a wreck.

"Are you finding everything you need?" Graham set aside his reading glasses and saw that Laura had returned to his table for the fourth time, seemingly to check on his progress.

"Do you have anything on Captain J. R. D. Forsyth of the Royal Jersey Militia?"

"Let me look," Laura replied.

Graham watched Laura walk away to consult the library's computer. She returned a few minutes later carrying five books, all with bubblegum pink sticky notes poking from between the pages like garish tongues.

"Excellent, thank you," Graham said. "I'm almost finished, in fact. Once again, I must congratulate the library on its collection. For a place so small," he said, glancing around, "it really is well stocked."

Laura beamed at him. "I'm glad," she said. "Do let me know if there's anything else I can do."

"Actually," Graham said as Laura began to turn to head back to the distribution desk, "there is." He had spoken without much thought and now felt committed. A wave of anxiety froze him for a second, but then he saw her smile once more and the words somehow came out. "I wonder if you'd like to have coffee with me sometime." His chest thumped. "If you're free, of course."

Laura's face showed many emotions in a busy split-second. There was surprise, as though this were the last thing she'd expected. She was flattered, he could tell, but there was something else; a kind of worry that seemed out of place. Graham expected that she would have thought such an invitation possible or even likely, but his request left her silent for so long that he began to chastise himself. She was new to Gorey, and he didn't know what kind of romantic situation she might already be involved in.

"Yes," she said finally, and laughed. "Sorry, it's been a while since anyone invited me out. I'd love to."

"Well, splendid," Graham said, finding his words far too formal as soon as he'd said them. "Great," he tried instead. "Let's set a time up tonight."

"I'll be working, but you can always text me." Laura glanced around for a moment, as if afraid of being seen giving her number to a library patron—a handsome, single one, at that. She quickly jotted it down and delivered one more sunny smile before returning to her work.

Graham quietly finished his research and returned the hardback books to the correct shelf. He strode out into the afternoon sunshine, feeling as good as he had in a long while. He considered his next step. He'd consult his junior colleagues back at the station. Perhaps one of them might teach him how to send a text.

Lillian paced angrily around the front room of her spacious town house, listening to the repeated tones of Charlotte's phone. There would be the requisite six rings, and then the all-too-familiar invitation to leave a voicemail. She almost screamed at the sound of Charlotte's recorded voice, promising that the call would be answered *just as soon as I am able*.

Deciding against leaving her fourth message of the day, Lillian considered violently pummelling one of the violet pillows that adorned her couch. Instead, she lit a cigarette and headed for the back bedroom where she found it therapeutic to yell at the two young volunteers she had drafted into working for Charlotte's campaign. They had already found that negotiating or debating with Lillian—or worse still, trying to placate her—was utterly futile and likely only to result in further outbursts of incandescent rage. They constantly kept an ear open for her footsteps on the stairs in order to brace themselves for an onslaught whilst feverishly discussing walking out on the job and whether or not they were brave enough to do it.

Back downstairs, Lillian called Charlotte again. "How in the name of Margaret Thatcher am I supposed to *help* you," she growled as the phone rang yet again, "if you won't even *speak* to me?"

Then the miraculous happened. "Lillian?" Charlotte said. "Sorry about that. Busy day. How are you?"

Rather uncharacteristically, the sheer relief of getting hold of her client after hours of radio silence prompted Lillian to take two deep breaths before answering. Her tone was measured and reasonable, which was a long way from how she truly felt. "I do hope," she said through gritted teeth, "that you'll be good enough to pick up the phone when the Prime Minister calls on election night to congratulate you."

Charlotte remained silent. She had anticipated a few moments of acidic fury from her campaign manager.

Unabashed, Lillian continued. "I demand that you come back to Market Ellestry right away. Your constituents need you. There's a lot to catch up on. Come home now, and I will deal with Don English. Then we can forget this little jaunt ever happened."

There were five seconds of resulting silence that did

nothing to lower Lillian's sky-high blood pressure. "I need a couple more days," Charlotte finally said. "I'm in the middle of something very important."

"Oh, good!" Lillian replied with feigned brightness. "I'm *so* glad it's important. Something about a *desk*, wasn't it? Doing a little *antiquing*, are we? Attending the odd *roadshow?*"

Charlotte ignored Lillian's sarcasm and got to the point. "Lilly, I need you to do something for me..."

When the call ended, Lillian sat on her couch feeling the anger coursing through her. Only after a couple of minutes did she look down and notice that her unconscious squeezing of the phone in her hand had left a sharp indentation in her palm.

Lillian stood. She had things to do, but she would do them in a moment. First, she returned upstairs to do the only thing that might help her mood: vent some more of her ceaseless fury upon the utterly petrified, blameless volunteers.

CHAPTER NINETEEN

FELIPE SAT DOWN slowly. He took off his glasses and poured himself another cup of thick, strong coffee from his battered, metal flask. He rubbed his eyes and blinked a few times, noting again just how tiring this close, exacting work could be. He had found sleep nearly impossible the night before. Instead of disturbing Rosa with his tossing and turning, he had headed down to his workshop to continue examining the Satterthwaite desk and plan the layers of varnish which would salve its unfortunate injuries.

The damage could have been worse. The wood was slightly bent but not chipped away, and there were no signs of structural faults to the desk itself. Such a heavy impact could have knocked the desk's delicate features out of alignment or cracked one of the internal braces which buttressed the piece. Happily, such severe damage had been avoided.

Felipe was deeply disturbed by what he had found the day before. Whenever he stood and took a moment's respite from his work, he found his thoughts bothering him. A repair that should have been the pleasure of a lifetime had now become a taxing, debilitating ordeal.

Still, he was making progress. The security guard's blood was all gone from the wood, and the area had been carefully but comprehensively disinfected. On arriving at his workshop just after four o'clock this morning, Felipe had once again checked the workshop's temperature and humidity. They had held steady overnight, and the initial layer of varnish had dried perfectly, just as he had hoped. The second layer was drying now, and he was already preparing the third, a darker tone of polish mixed from three sources. He would need only a tiny amount, but every layer was important. If the underlying work wasn't perfect, the newly varnished corner would reflect light incorrectly and have a different feel under his fingertips.

As he drank his coffee, Felipe's mind wandered yet again. His were painful memories. Eventually, he shrugged them off. There was work to do, and this desk demanded his very best. He knelt by the damaged corner once more and applied a third layer of varnish with the care and attentiveness of a heart surgeon. During those moments, nothing in the world existed but the damaged surface and his brush. He watched every hair, every movement, every millimetre of the application. After fifteen minutes, he stood slowly, rubbing his aching knees, and found himself reminded again of the strange discovery this fine desk had brought.

Whilst the layer dried, he made more coffee and searched on his phone for information on the desk's former owner. He learnt that Sir Thomas Hughes was a hero to some and a villain to many. One photo of him working at the Satterthwaite desk survived. Hughes' hair awry, his back to the camera, he was working amidst piles of papers strewn all over, whilst a black spaniel, seated by the chair, looked up imploringly at his frantically busy master. In that single snapshot, Hughes seemed to be a man possessed.

"Was it guilt?" Felipe asked the photograph, in the silence of his workshop. "Is *that* what was driving you?" He pictured Hughes trying desperately to atone for a life of compromises and selfishness, an existence motivated far too much by greed and not nearly enough by compassion. He pulled a piece of paper from his pocket, and as he read what he had found once again, he reminded himself just how complex a man Sir Thomas must have been.

The fourth coat of varnish went on smoothly, raising the damaged layer a little further. Once it dried, it would offer a solid base for the next coat as he built up the marred section of wood. Absentmindedly, Felipe reached for his flask. He needed more coffee. Finding the container empty, he turned toward the tiny kitchenette he'd built in the corner of the workshop and set the flask in the sink before reaching into the cupboard for a bag of coffee beans. He heard a rip as a seam in his workman's jacket came undone.

Rosa knocked on the workshop door.

"*Si, mi amor?*" he said, as he always did.

"Are you busy, Felipe?" she replied through the door.

"Just stitching my jacket, my love."

"There's a phone call for you. It's about the desk, but they would not say more," she told him.

Felipe frowned and opened the door, itself a product of his fine craftsmanship. "The desk?" he asked and took the cordless landline from his wife. She shrugged. She had known Felipe for enough years to know when a project was weighing heavily on him, and she knew this desk was providing a unique challenge even for a man as skilled as he. Felipe smiled at her fondly and closed the door.

"Hello?"

"Mr. Barrios, I'm grateful for a moment of your time." It was a strange voice, slightly metallic and false, with no sense of gender at all. "I understand that you're repairing the Satterthwaite desk."

"That's correct," Felipe responded guardedly. "Who is speaking, please?"

"I'm an antique collector and a big Satterthwaite fan. Could I possibly arrange a visit so that I could see the desk for a few moments? It would be a huge privilege. Would this afternoon be convenient?"

Felipe's frown deepened. "Ah, no. I'm afraid not. Visitors are not allowed in the workshop. And this is a sensitive matter, I'm sure you understand," he said.

"Quite so," the voice said. Felipe thought it most odd that it contained neither male nor female markers. It was more like speaking with a machine. It was chilling, and it did not dispose him well to this unexpected caller, who hadn't properly introduced themselves. "I wonder, how are the repairs progressing?" the caller asked.

There seemed no harm in answering honestly. "Quite well. The damage was not as severe as it might have been. But, I must ask again, who is this speaking?"

"That's good news. Very good," the voice said. "Did you find anything unusual?"

"What do you mean?"

"Something inside the desk?" the voice asked.

There were perhaps ten seconds of silence. "No. Nothing," Felipe finally said.

"I understand," the voice intoned. "It is not something

that is easy to discuss on the phone. Perhaps we could meet this afternoon? Outside your workshop, if you prefer."

Felipe found his courage once more. "I'm afraid that's impossible. I am fully committed to repairing the desk, and I don't know you at all. You have not told me who you are."

"I believe," the voice said, the tone changing slightly, "that you'll find meeting with me worth your while."

"No," Felipe reiterated. "I'm sorry. I'm not able to help you."

"Come now, Mr. Barrios. I have an offer to make you. Shall we say," the voice proposed, "thirty thousand pounds for the letter?"

Felipe's eyes widened. "There is no letter," he said steadily. "I don't know who you are, but there's been a misunderstanding."

"Ah," the voice said. "Well, just so there's no misunderstanding, shall we call it forty thousand?"

Madre de Dios... "There is," Felipe repeated, "no letter."

There was a metallic sigh. "Very well, but please take time to reconsider. It would be in your best interest. I will be in touch. In the meantime, good luck with your repairs." *Click.*

Felipe dropped the phone from his ear and carefully placed it on the workbench. He leant against the side, the heels of his hands taking his weight. He bent his head as he took in the implications of the call. At length, he returned to polishing the desk, using the focus required to block out his anxieties, but not before re-checking that all his windows were bolted and the door firmly locked.

Felipe worked late again, and by two o'clock in the morning, the fifth layer of polish was drying. A cat mewled loudly outside, and he heard a scratching, scrabbling sound from the back of the workshop. "No mice for you tonight, Leo?" he said.

He paused for a second, trying to calculate just how much coffee he had drunk during this long, complicated day. "Too much," he muttered, but he knew that he had to work. His painstaking restoration of the desk was the only way to occupy his troubled mind.

There was a creak behind him. He started to turn, but too late he felt a tremendous *thump* on the back of his head. His forehead crashed into the counter, and his knees collapsed beneath him. The weight of his lower body forced his head back, and as gravity exerted its force, his chin again hit the countertop. The floor came up to meet him and there he lay prone, helpless, a small trickle of blood zig-zagging from the corner of his mouth down to the tile of the workshop floor.

CHAPTER TWENTY

JIM ROACH SHIFTED in his swivel chair behind the reception desk so that he could place his aching ankle on the lowest shelf to his left. The ice packs were helping, but he couldn't remember taking a more ferocious whack to the shin than the "defensive tackle" he had endured a few nights before.

"Still in the wars, Jim?" Sergeant Harding asked as she came out from her small office.

"Didn't even get a foul out of it," Roach complained. "If the referee could have seen a replay, he'd have given the guy a yellow card. No doubt about it." The bruising had peaked in the form of an angry, dark purple oval.

Janice sipped her coffee. "Anything interesting happen last night?" she asked.

"Mrs. Hollingsworth, over by the library, called to report a 'suspicious character' again, but I'm not certain she's not seeing things. She is ninety, after all."

"What kind of character?" Janice said.

"She doesn't say exactly. But I can't not go out, can I?

Not after the break-in at the museum. She's called two nights last week and three this. I keep driving out there, only to find the place deserted, and no signs of anyone, suspicious or otherwise. All I see is the new librarian closing up for the night."

Janice shrugged. "Perhaps that's it. She got confused. Old age always comes at a bad time. It's not unlike some of our older residents to become concerned by people they don't recognise."

"I'm thinking of getting Barnwell to stake out the area and deal with it once and for all."

"You'll really put the wind up her if you do that," Janice leant over his shoulder. "So, what's on the menu this morning?"

"I'm going to re-read the pathology report on the night watchman at the museum," Roach said. It was frustrating them all that the evidence relating to the break-in and Nobby Norris' death pointed nowhere in particular.

"The DI's giving you some more forensics practice, is he?"

"I guess," Roach demurred. In truth, he had come close to begging Graham to let him read and digest the report.

"So, what do we finally know about poor old Nobby?"

Roach finished a note he was making on a legal pad. "He had a heart condition, though it seems undiagnosed and untreated," Roach told her. "Tomlinson found signs of hardened arteries, and the levels of ATP in his blood indicated that he was under tremendous stress when he died. But here's the thing, we can't say how or even if anyone else was involved in his death. Nobby could have just happened to keel over on the same night the museum was burgled. A coincidence."

Janice examined the file briefly. "I thought the DI was training us not to believe in coincidences? And we did see someone on the CCTV," she reminded him.

"Yeah, you're right. But we don't even have a suspect. We're nowhere in this case."

"Are there signs of a struggle?" Janice asked.

"There's no bruising to indicate defensive wounds or that Nobby might have hit anyone," Roach said. "Just the one injury to his left temple, where he hit the desk. But that wasn't enough to kill him. It was the heart attack that did for him."

Janice sat on one of the plastic chairs opposite the reception desk. "Alright, let's think about it. Say that we're burgling the museum, and we know there's a guard. What do we do about him?"

Roach closed the file. "Surprise him, tie him up, and gag him."

"Incapacitate him, in other words," Janice said.

"Right. Then burgle the museum's treasures to our hearts' content."

"But say for a moment that Nobby wasn't in the mood to be tied up, and he fought back."

"But there's no evidence. We can't prove that," Roach warned.

"Hmm. Are we sure there was only one intruder?" Janice asked.

Roach was in the middle of answering, "We're really not sure of anything," when the red phone rang. "Oh, hell." He lifted the receiver and grabbed his pen. "Gorey Police." He wrote quickly and flashed Janice a worried look. "Get the boss," he mouthed.

DI Graham swore. That reputation he'd been gaining for engineering a big drop in the local crime rate had just been shot to pieces. "I'm not far from the crime scene now. Meet me there, would you? Have Roach hold the fort."

"I should say, sir," Janice told him, "that Constable Roach is very keen to attend."

The DI's reply was delayed by some laboured breathing. Harding asked, "Are you *running* to the crime scene, sir?"

"Yes, if you must know," Graham panted. "And I wish the call had come in a little more than a few minutes after I'd finished one of Mrs. Taylor's quite magnificent breakfasts."

Janice pictured the detective inspector dodging morning shoppers on Gorey's high street, having already pelted down the hill from the White House Inn. "I'll be at the victim's workshop in a few minutes, sir. See you there," she said.

"Roger and out." Graham cursed the weight of the bacon, eggs, and black pudding he had consumed not fifteen minutes earlier and pressed on until he saw the sign for Steadman & Barrios. "Of all the places," he muttered, "for a violent incident. Not a pub, or a nightclub, but the workshop of a high-class furniture maker." He puffed and made a mental note to think again about buying a car. Laura hadn't hesitated in that regard, he'd noticed.

When he reached the workshop, Sergeant Harding had already arrived in the marked police vehicle. Graham caught his breath and waved the sergeant inside.

"The ambulance left a few minutes ago, sir," Harding told him.

"Good. Where's the wife?" he asked.

"In the ambulance with Mr. Barrios. I spoke with the dispatcher again and... well, it doesn't sound good, sir."

"Damn," Graham said. "What the *hell* is going on? Send Barnwell over to the hospital to get a witness statement from Mrs. Barrios." The workshop door was open. Graham noted its elegant finish and precise fit as he entered the large, open-plan room.

"The desk, again," he said.

"Here for repairs, sir," Janice pointed out. "Mr. Barrios' wife told the ambulance crew that he was working on it last night. But he never came up to bed. She found him this morning."

The rest of what happened was obvious by the large, darkened pool of blood on the workshop's stone floor. "Head wound?" Graham guessed.

"Yes, sir." Janice was on hold with the emergency dispatcher, who was relaying the initial reports from the ambulance crew. She listened for a moment and frowned. "They suspect a fractured skull. Blunt force trauma. He's gone into cardiac arrest twice already. I have to say they don't sound hopeful."

"Which ambulance crew is it?" Graham asked.

"Same crew as attended the museum."

"Let me speak to them. Can I be patched through?" Janice spoke to the dispatcher and handed Graham the phone. "Alan? What can you tell me?"

"The patient took a severe blow to the back of the head," the paramedic said. Graham heard no siren in the background. Experienced medics knew that it scared their patients, and it was usually only used in heavy traffic. "Seems to have been hit with a large metal or wooden object. He's got a severe skull fracture. Sue thinks he's likely to have intra-cerebral bleeding. He was unconscious for an extended period before being found. At least a couple of hours was Sue's guess. His heart's stopped twice in the ambulance, but we got him back both times. Still, it's touch and go."

Graham ended the call and then walked around the broad, dried circle of blood to examine the desk. "*You* again," he said. "What *is* it about you?"

"Sir?" Janice asked, feeling lost.

"Nobby hit his head," Graham explained, indicating the damaged corner, "right here, and whilst it wasn't the end of him, it played its part. Now we have Felipe Barrios working on the same desk, and now *he's* in hospital with a cracked skull. *Why?*"

"An attempted robbery?" Janice tried. "I mean, it's clearly very valuable."

Graham stood, hands on hips, and regarded the Satterthwaite desk. It seemed tiny by modern standards, fit for a more elegant time when the people were a little smaller, and quality was less often confused with quantity. "Hardly. Whoever it was incapacitated the victim and then left without the desk," Graham pointed out. "There's no sign of any attempt to even move it."

Harding's phone rang. "Yes?" she said. "Okay, I'll ask him." She turned to Graham, who was staring, perplexed, at the desk. "Constable Roach requests permission to attend the crime scene, sir. And perhaps I should go to the hospital. Talk to Mrs. Barrios."

"Yes, do that Harding. Tell Roach to direct calls to St. Helier, and have Barnwell get back to the station ASAP."

Janice spoke again into the phone. "Roach says he's already in touch with Adam Harris-Watts and suggests bringing him here to see if he can help us."

"Oh God, alright," Graham grumbled. "But tell him to warn Harris-Watts about the blood would you? That curator is a fragile sort."

CHAPTER TWENTY-ONE

CONSTABLE ROACH EXAMINED the desk as though searching for a hidden code within its very construction. "Interesting," he said, more than once. "Very interesting."

Graham indulged him as far as he could, given the circumstances. They had no murder weapon, no suspect, and no reason for Felipe Barrios' attack. He put this to Roach, who seized the moment.

"Well, the attack seems to have taken place in the dead of night, when Felipe was alone in the workshop," Roach pointed out. "The attacker probably knew they wouldn't be disturbed. That constitutes an opportunity."

"Yes obviously, but for whom? We have no idea who, why, or how." From outside, Graham heard the sounds of Adam Harris-Watts' visceral reaction to the large pool of blood. He rolled his eyes. "We'll check on him in a minute," Graham said. "Carry on, Constable."

"We need to find the weapon that was used to attack the victim," Roach said next, looking around the workroom.

"No success there," said Graham, who had spent the previous forty minutes memorising and minutely examining every tool and object on the walls, in drawers, and on the workbench. "So, what about motive?"

Roach shook his head. "Must be something to do with the desk. That's the connection."

"Certainly. We've now had two incidents relating to it. But what's the significance?" Roach looked at him and shrugged.

Harris-Watts reappeared, looking gaunt and unsteady. "Sorry," he said, for what seemed like the twentieth time. "I'm rather out of my element with all this crime scene stuff."

"We'd like you to focus on the desk," Graham said. "And tell us if you notice anything unusual."

Doing his best to pull his attention away from the sickening evidence of brutal injury on the workshop floor, Harris-Watts examined the Satterthwaite desk with an expert eye. "Felipe was obviously making progress on the repairs," he said. "A good portion of the polish is in place." His mind focused now, Harris-Watts stepped around the desk and examined the rear, and then the underside. Roach watched him, envious of the older man's knowledge. "Nothing seems amiss," Harris-Watts said, and then reached for the brass handle to open the main drawer.

"No!" Both Graham and Roach leaped to intervene before the curator placed a naked finger on the desk.

"Sorry, sorry. Of course," Harris-Watts stammered as he put on the latex gloves Graham offered him. He leant forward, bending over. He ran his fingertips along the drawer at the front of the desk and then reached underneath and did the same.

His response, a pained, stunned gasp, immediately brought Graham to his side. "What? What is it?"

Harris-Watts pressed the mechanism on the underside of the drawer. They all heard the "thunk" from deep inside the desk. Harris-Watts pulled the drawer out. He could barely bring himself to utter the words. "*I've found it.* At last. Of all the... " He looked at Graham, his eyes wide. "There's a secret compartment! It's what Satterthwaite was known for. We always suspected there was one here. But no one could find the mechanism that opened it. Even Charlotte Hughes couldn't find it."

"Who?" Graham asked.

"Charlotte Hughes, the daughter of the original owner. Said the family looked for it many times without success. She was here a few days ago. Paid for the repairs. It was very kind of her. The museum wouldn't have been able to afford them otherwise."

Roach fizzed with excitement. "Is there anything inside?"

The curator showed the two officers the peculiar, but empty little nook at the very back. "No," he said glumly. "Nothing."

But Graham's mind was racing. "Nothing *now*," he cautioned. "But I'm betting there *was.*"

🌍

Photographing and documenting the crime scene took another hour during which Graham regularly called the hospital for an update. These situations were always deeply frustrating for investigating officers. The victim was perhaps the only person in the world with definitive information on the nature of the attack and its perpetrator, but Graham didn't know if Felipe Barrios would ever speak again.

Roach busied himself chronicling the desk, peppering the pale-faced Harris-Watts all the while with a sequence of questions which made him sound a far more accomplished and thoughtful investigator than his lowly rank might imply. Increasingly, Graham had been bringing him along to crime scenes and never regretted it, although Roach did allow his enthusiasm to boil over now and then. It took the occasional steadying glance from the DI to remind Roach that exciting as all this might well be, detective work was a serious, sometimes deadly business. To emphasise his point, Graham's phone rang with news from the hospital. It was Janice. He knew immediately that the news wasn't good.

"I'm sorry, sir. Mr. Barrios' injuries were too severe. They did everything they could, but the doctors pronounced him dead a few moments ago. Dr. Tomlinson says he'll get to work shortly."

Graham pursed his lips and his knuckles whitened as he gripped his phone. He stomped around in a broad circle for a few moments, wincing at the tragic, pointless *unfairness* of such a death. He punched Tomlinson's number into his phone.

"Can you give me any preliminaries, Marcus?"

"Nothing yet, old boy," Tomlinson told him. "Look, I've got some paperwork to do here, and then I'll begin the post-mortem proper."

"Please make a start as soon as you're able," Graham snapped. "And get me everything you can on the likely murder weapon. This place is full of tools but there are no obvious signs that any of them was used. Shape, size, anything. Soon as you can." He hung up.

Roach eyed his boss nervously. It wasn't unlike him to

take these cases very personally. He watched Graham staring at the desk, as if willing the masterpiece to explain itself. "He's gone, then, sir?" he finally said to the silent Graham.

"A few minutes ago," Graham scowled. "No CCTV. No witnesses," he continued, mostly to himself. "No nothing."

Lillian awoke and immediately looked at her phone. Blast! It was gone 11 AM, and she'd had no phone calls or texts from Charlotte. Lillian reached for the packet of cigarettes by her bed but groaned and slammed it back down when she realised she'd have to lean out of the window to have a smoke, or worse, get up and go outside. In the mid-morning light, her room was small but bright, her view of the English Channel glorious. The water glistened in the sunshine. She could see a container ship crawling across the horizon.

Lillian had arrived the previous evening. She had checked in to the White House Inn, having been assured it was the best guesthouse on the island. Noting the rubber plant and the oak paneling in the reception area, she considered the recommendation to bode poorly for the other accommodations on Jersey. Grousing, she had made her way to her room, determined to waste no time in getting hold of Charlotte. She needed to get her off this godforsaken island as soon as possible, but she'd had zero success in contacting her charge.

Lillian stared at the ceiling for a few moments, before rising. She dressed, winding a purple scarf around her neck in order to guard herself against the chill of the spring morning. She was on a mission to protect her latest and brightest client. On this bucolic March morning, her mission was to save Charlotte Hughes from disaster.

She tapped a message out on her phone. It sounded a lot more charitable than she felt. *Charlotte, where are you, child?*

CHAPTER TWENTY-TWO

JANICE HAD FOUND Rosa Barrios still trembling, surrounded by three of her friends. They were sitting in stunned silence in one of the hospital's quiet waiting rooms. Although Barnwell had taken an initial statement, he had remained aloof from the group and was relieved to see Janice approaching the room.

"Sergeant," Barnwell said simply, stepping out into the hallway to meet her.

"Pretty grim, eh, Constable?" she said consolingly.

"He was well-liked with no known enemies," Barnwell reported. Being around grieving people put him in a distinctly thoughtful frame of mind. He was looking forward to leaving the hospital behind and returning to the station. He handed over a very brief witness statement. "She was upset," was all he said.

"Okay, Constable, thanks. The DI wants you back at the station. Roach is at the crime scene. I'll call if I need you, and you do the same, alright?"

Barnwell nodded and went on his way, happy to be out of the hospital and in the fresh air.

Rosa Barrios made to stand as Janice entered, but the sergeant waved her back down. "Mrs. Barrios, I'm Sergeant Janice Harding," she said. "I'm here to help you if you feel up to speaking to me." She politely requested that Rosa's three friends leave them for the moment.

Rosa was a small woman with big brown eyes and hair pulled back in a bun. "I want to help," she said. "I just don't understand..." Tears welled up but were forced back down again. She would be strong at this moment, and when the time was right, she would allow her grief to wash over her again. "I told the other man everything. The big officer," she clarified.

Janice almost smiled. "Mrs. Barrios, tell me about your husband. You'd been married for, what, forty years?"

"Yes, we were both born and raised in San Marcos. We met on the beach when we were just teenagers." Rosa smiled at the memory. "We came here when we were first married."

Janice held eye contact with Rosa, building an intimacy with her that would encourage her to speak. "San Marcos is where exactly?

"In Central America. We came to Jersey in 1978."

"Why did you leave your home country? Were you not happy there?"

Rosa's face darkened. "San Marcos came upon very difficult times. The forces from the neighbouring state of Suriguay assaulted our capital and took control. Eventually, we had to flee." Rosa looked down at her hands in her lap for a long moment. Janice waited for the older woman to resume her story. "We lived through horrible years that followed the 'revolution.' That's what they called it, the *junta*'s propagandists." Rosa's face hardened. She spat out the word, "junta." "It was a military coup. A period of great difficulty. Felipe's parents were professors and were constantly harassed." Rosa's mouth turned down at the corners, paying no attention to Janice as she stared into space, lost in her memories.

"Felipe had dreamed of college, even as the 'education department' closed down almost every institute of higher learning in our country. There was a new government-sponsored curriculum. Dissent wasn't tolerated. Students were encouraged to inform on their classmates and even on their teachers. Many professors were taken away for 're-education'! They never came back." Rosa clasped her hands to her chest and rocked gently. "There were rumours of secret political meetings at Felipe's parents' apartment. They were being watched and eventually they were arrested in the dead of night." Tears rolled down Rosa's face.

"Poor Felipe! His parents were idealistic and brave, always defying the authoritarian thugs who had come to dominate our country. I was in awe of them! My family was poor, uneducated, but Felipe's parents taught me that democracy was not a radical, unhinged, sinful experiment, that social mobility was my birthright!" Rosa's lips quivered, and she raised the handkerchief in her hand up to her mouth. Janice leant in and put her hand on the older woman's forearm, concern etched on her face.

Rosa calmed herself after a few sobs and spoke again. "Felipe said we had to leave, but I didn't want to. I wanted to stay with my family, but he insisted. He said that it would be worse if we stayed. His parents had always warned him it would be so. We used our last money to board a fishing trawler in the middle of the night. There were so many people, little children, babies. We were all crying. I was so scared we would drown. But somehow, the boat carried us to Jamaica. I have never prayed so hard in my life."

"And how did you end up here? From Jamaica to Jersey?"

"An embassy official took pity on us. He allowed us to make one phone call. Felipe called Mr. Steadman. He worked so hard to get us here, paid money, filled in forms, and hired lawyers for us. We made it, and we've been here ever since."

"Mr. Steadman owned the business Felipe now has?"

"Yes, they met when Felipe was a boy. Back then, San Marcos was popular with tourists, and they would come to fish and snorkel. They liked to taste the best rum in Central America. Mr. Steadman, just two days into his holiday, was found on the beach with blood coming from a wound on his leg. Felipe was the first to reach him and understood enough English to realise what had happened." Rosa looked at Janice knowingly. "Sea snake."

"Felipe cared for him as an intense fever took hold of *Señor* Steadman. He was his constant companion through the pain and tremors. He brought Mr. Steadman water and broth, and when Mr. Steadman's fever passed, he fed him meals. He never left his side. Later, Mr. Steadman said he owed his life entirely to Felipe. He promised to help him in any way he could, and he was true to his word. We owe him our lives. But it was a terrible time.

"When we arrived here on the island, exhausted, heartsick, and cold, Felipe was told that his parents had been executed by the regime. For many weeks, Felipe spoke to no one except me and Mr. Steadman. It took a while, but eventually he began to explore Jersey and settle here. He polished his English by taking courses at the local college, and Mr. Steadman taught him woodworking and cabinetmaking. He eventually allowed Felipe to work on his own projects, and just before Mr. Steadman died, Felipe completed a beautiful dining table set, his first major commission. Oh, it was wonderful! So beautiful! Felipe's true passion, though, was repairing old furniture. He was humbled to be working on a piece designed by Ezekiel Satterthwaite."

"Did he tell you anything about the desk? Was there anything unusual about it?" Janice asked, bringing out her notebook.

"He was very excited," Rosa said, her face brightening before almost immediately clouding again, "but something strange did happen yesterday. There was a phone call. About the desk. That's all I know. The person didn't say who they were and Felipe didn't come up to the house again." She paused for a moment and looked closely at the sergeant. Her tired, brown eyes were puffy now from crying. "It wasn't just a robbery?"

Janice was making a discreet note. "I'm not sure what you mean, Mrs. Barrios," she said, setting down her iPad.

"The person who came to the workshop last night. The one who attacked him. They were... looking for something, weren't they?" she asked, focusing intently on Janice.

"We don't know at this point, Mrs. Barrios, but I can assure you we will do everything in our power to find out who did this to your husband."

Rosa reached out and took Janice's hand. She had short, broad fingers that were extremely soft, but her grip was surprisingly firm. "God knows," she said slowly, "what happened to my Felipe. I pray that he will guide you and your colleagues to uncover the truth," she added, tears coming again.

Janice never quite knew what to say when burdened by such hopes. "We'll do everything we can," she said in the end. "DI Graham is one of the best investigators in the country." She held onto Rosa's hand for a long, quiet moment, praying that her boss would once again prove himself equal to the task.

Graham met Janice at the hospital. She found him in a dark and brooding mood that she suspected wasn't due only to the unnecessary and tragic death of Felipe Barrios. Although Graham had never said so, Janice harboured a belief that hospitals held dreadful associations for the DI. She knew better than to quiz such a private person, but more than once, she had found herself speculating at what might lie in Graham's past.

She recounted everything that Rosa had told her, including the mysterious phone call. Graham's face darkened as she spoke. "Poor guy," he said when she'd finished. "To go through all that and then get taken out by some animal." They walked silently along the hospital corridors to the morgue.

"Marcus?" Graham said as soon the two officers saw him.

"Sorry, old boy," the pathologist said again. "I know you had hopes on this one."

Graham shrugged just slightly. "What can you tell me?"

"It's early days but definitely blunt force trauma, as we thought," Marcus explained. "A long, relatively thin metal object. My guess is a file or maybe a sharpening steel. In any event, he was hit pretty hard from behind by a right-handed assailant."

"What else?" Graham said, memorising the details and bringing to mind his observations from the workshop.

"He was struck once and then left on the ground. The

victim took a well-aimed and ferocious thwack to his head. I can't know if the attacker meant to kill him or simply incapacitate him.

"Could it have been a woman?"

"With a tool like that, yes. It's not heavy, and with sufficient force and precise placement, it could be deadly wielded by a male or a female.

Janice interjected. "So they broke in quietly and attacked him, unawares? Or perhaps," she tried, "Felipe knew the attacker, invited them in, and they hit him when his back was turned?"

"Either of those explanations is possible," Tomlinson said. "Based on our preliminary findings, you understand."

"What about the injury?" Graham said.

Marcus showed him a diagram of a skull, with a star-shaped fracture radiating out from an impact point above the right ear. "The bleeding was very sudden and severe." Tomlinson ringed the diagram with his closed pen. "But because the skull is a rigid container, the blood has nowhere to go except out through the small cut made by the impact, or down the *foramen magnum*."

"The where?" Harding asked.

"The hole in the bottom of the skull," Tomlinson replied, tapping the back of his own neck. "Through which the spinal cord passes. Everything gets forced down that way. There's no other escape route. It causes herniation, an increase in pressure. This shuts down breathing and other vital functions. The results aren't usually survivable."

Harding, feeling distinctly queasy, stepped out for a moment whilst Graham listened to the rest of Tomlinson's findings. "Are there any similarities," Graham asked, his voice grave, "to the death of Mr. Norris at the museum?"

Tomlinson shook his head. "No, other than the obvious proximity of the desk."

"There was a hidden compartment in one of the drawers."

Marcus looked closely at Graham. "Compartment?"

"Yes. Adam Harris-Watts was quite beside himself about it. The maker, Satterthwaite, was known for incorporating hidden drawers in some of his pieces, but no one had been able to find one in this particular desk until now."

"It was empty, wasn't it?" Tomlinson said.

"Yes it was... How did you know it would be?" Graham asked.

Marcus led him from the room. "Come with me, Detective Inspector." They changed out of their surgical scrubs. "I need to introduce you to our new forensics expert."

Tomlinson led Graham to his own car, parked outside the hospital's front entrance. "It's easier just to show you. Young Mr. Oxley has something that you really need to see."

CHAPTER TWENTY-THREE

TOMLINSON LED GRAHAM through the double doors and into the forensics lab. It was a place the DI had been to many times before, but Tomlinson's eagerness gave the lab an air of expectancy. "A Dr. Simon Oxley. New chap," Tomlinson had told him on the way over. "Based at Cambridge University but loaned out to the Metropolitan Police for consulting on cases that need his expertise. Miranda happened to be in a meeting with him when she took my call. He popped straight over."

Dr. Miranda Weiss was the Head of Forensics for the Jersey Police. She resided on the mainland, so Tomlinson sometimes found himself doing double duty as a forensics investigator, or at least overseeing some of the more rarefied tasks that landed on his mortuary table. They were tasks he usually relished—intellectually challenging and generally cutting edge.

"Did you know him whilst you were at the Met?" Graham shook his head. Tomlinson continued, "Anyhow, he arrived a couple of hours ago. Smartest young man I've met in a while." Tomlinson tapped his temple. *"Listen to* him, David. Don't let his looks deceive you," he said, ushering Graham into the room.

"Looks?" Graham asked, noticing the faint chemical smell as he walked into the lab. "How do you mean?" He turned to find an extremely tall, fresh-faced young man smiling down at him.

"How do you do, DI Graham?" the youthful-looking giant asked, extending his hand. "I've heard a great deal about you." Simon Oxley was nearly seven feet tall, with an enthusiastic, genuine smile, and glinting, excited eyes that were magnified by thick, steel-rimmed glasses. "I'm hoping I can be of some assistance," he said, as Graham's hand met his own. The young man's grip was surprisingly dainty given his intimidating height.

"I'm hoping so, too," Graham said. "Marcus seems to think highly of you. We've got ourselves a very special and particular case here."

"Felipe Barrios. Yes," Oxley said soberly.

"It was the jacket he was wearing when he was attacked that proved to be of the greatest interest," Tomlinson said. He took Graham's arm and steered the DI to an examination table. On it lay a single piece of clothing. "We're hoping that this jacket is going to teach us *why* Barrios was killed," Tomlinson said.

Oxley showed them two large, glossy photographs. One contained an image of a single piece of paper, the other, a curled-up Polaroid. Graham could see it had originally been black and white but had faded to shades of grey and pink. Oxley placed them next to the jacket on the metal table. "You found these in the pocket?" Graham surmised. It wasn't a staggering feat of detective work. The jacket and the paper pictured in the photograph were almost completely soaked in blood. The Polaroid was relatively unscathed.

"The originals," Oxley explained, "are in cold storage now. We're focusing on the paper that contains the handwriting." Graham looked carefully at the photograph with the handwritten paper. There were only three legible sections that he could see, only a handful of words, he estimated.

"We're going to use a process called lyophilisation to freeze-dry the document and then sublimate the frozen water present in the blood's plasma by turning it to vapour."

Graham stared at him briefly. "Okay."

"Dr. Oxley is an expert on document retrieval, storage, and reconstruction," Tomlinson told him. "When paper gets wet, as this has with blood, the best method of restoring it is to freeze away the water present, leaving just the original material behind."

"And the remainder of the blood, presumably," Graham said, dubiously.

"Yes, that's true, but blood comprises fifty-five percent plasma, of which ninety-two percent is water, so we should see a great improvement in the legibility of this document."

"It will take at least a day, perhaps two," Oxley said, "even with the new technique we're using. But we've had a very pleasing success rate." He beamed.

"After that, we'll use an X-ray scanner. Hopefully, we'll be able to see what the paper was about," Tomlinson added. Graham could see the pathologist had warmed to this new and interesting project. "Tell him about the papyrus from that Roman villa, Simon."

Oxley was all set to launch into what Graham was certain would be a fascinating tale, but he was far too engrossed in the murder investigation to pay it any mind at this moment. "Tell me about this," he said, standing over Felipe's blood-soaked jacket, his index finger pointing to the metal tabletop.

"This jacket is one of a kind that a carpenter or painter might wear," Tomlinson told him. "Lots of pockets for brushes and tools, and a comfortable fit so his arms aren't constrained. It isn't the kind of thing you'd wear outside the workshop," Marcus said. "And, at first glance, I saw no earthly reason to think that it was anything other than what it appeared to be. But then I noticed this," he said. Slowly, Tomlinson used tweezers to lift some fabric where the stitching at the seam under the armpit had been removed to leave a three-inch opening. "See here? The fabric has been freshly sewn. We found the letter inside the lining of the sleeve, presumably placed there through this gap and quite recently too."

Graham peered at the photo of the document once more. According to the scale placed next to it, the paper was letter-sized, and the few fragments that remained free of blood showed handwriting in a very neat, educated script. Graham's first impression was that it might be a college graduation certificate. "So, what is it?" he asked Oxley.

"My doctoral thesis discussed methods of analysing documents that were illegible or damaged," Simon told him, peering down at the DI and the document.

"Very high-end stuff," Tomlinson whispered to Graham. "X-rays and such. You wouldn't believe the things they can do."

"Yes, but what is it?" Graham repeated. He wasn't as enamoured by the scientific brilliance of the process as much as he was by its outcome.

"I'm not sure yet. This is a very difficult case, but I do expect to be able to glean something from the remnants."

THE CASE OF THE MISSING LETTER   147

Dr. Oxley handled the photograph with a soft, measured touch, his long, pale, soft fingers lingering over the image. Graham imagined those hands at the keyboards of a church organ perhaps, or expertly wielding a surgeon's scalpel. "After the water has been extracted, we will have a clearer picture of what we are dealing with. There are other layered techniques we can use to recover the contents of the document if necessary, including ascertaining the chemical composition of the ink."

"Something in which," Tomlinson explained, "Simon is also a noted expert."

"Gradually," Oxley said, "we should be able to build a picture of what this paper originally communicated."

Graham looked up at the man, once again doubting that someone who couldn't possibly have yet turned thirty had already gained such a reputation, not to mention a doctorate in the sciences. "How long will it take?"

"As I mentioned earlier, a day or so."

Graham sighed. "Is there anything you can tell me now?"

Oxley looked down at the bloodied paper. "We can make a few deductions, yes."

"I'm interested to hear what you have to say," Graham persisted.

Oxley set down the photo and reached for his laptop on the opposite table. "The author was highly educated, probably in the nineteen-forties. We can tell this from aspects of his letter formation. There's also a rigour to the penmanship that spoke of many patient hours of practice, probably under the watchful eye of a strict tutor."

Tomlinson gave Graham a wink. "Told you he was good, didn't I?"

Oxley continued. "The author was a meticulous person,

someone for whom the effort of writing a letter by hand was considered a worthwhile investment." Graham stared at the photographed document again.

"The words we can read suggest that it is a letter of some kind. The formal, rather archaic language supports the idea that the author was educated and disciplined, and I also suggest that this was a letter to an acquaintance, possibly a friend, more than a business or official communication. All of this helps us to date the letter, even before we receive the results of chemical analysis on the ink and the paper."

"So when do you think it was written?"

"My guess is that the paper, and this is only a guess, mind, is probably around fifty years old. It is well preserved, and I suspect was only handled fairly infrequently."

"That would fit with what you were saying about the compartment, wouldn't it, David?" Tomlinson suggested.

Graham looked at him, his lips pursed. The pathologist continued. "Once we get the results back, we'll know where the paper came from. Almost down to the individual *forest*."

"Extraordinary," Graham breathed. "But how will that help us?"

"We can home in on the location where the letter was written," Simon Oxley said.

"And how many of us," Tomlinson suggested, "would use an expression like, 'long have endured,' as the author does here?"

"Sophisticated grammatical structure is a hallmark both of high-class education and social standing. This was almost certainly written by someone in a position of power. And there's something else," Oxley told Graham. "Do you see these tiny cursive features on the letters 's' and 'p'?"

Graham looked more closely. There were curious, almost affected little swirls.

"What do they signify?" Graham said.

"Well, here I'm beginning to speculate," Oxley admitted, "but I would say there's a better-than-even chance that our author was raised in a Spanish-speaking country."

"Could Felipe have written it himself?" Graham asked.

Oxley shrugged his thin shoulders. "I doubt it. Felipe was entirely too young to have been educated using this kind of language and script. Plus, given that he secreted the letter on his person, it's much more likely that it was written by someone who was important to him in some way."

"Tell me about the photograph you found." Graham said.

"I'll go and get it from the freezer," Tomlinson offered. "You can take this with you," he said when he came back. "Looks like it's from the seventies to me. It is less compromised and has absorbed less of the blood than the letter." He gave Graham a bag inside which a monochromatic photo clearly showed a beach scene with two men and a woman squinting toward the camera. One man shielded his eyes, his face half in shadow. The woman was fair, her shoulder length hair lying in shiny waves. She was wearing white starfish earrings and a matching necklace.

Graham stared at the photo, staying absolutely still. He was silent for so long that the two scientists exchanged a curious glance. Tomlinson let the silence reign, aware that the longer DI David Graham considered a problem, the better his answer tended to be.

Finally, Graham brought out his phone. "Excuse me a moment." He speed-dialled a number. "Ah, Constable Roach. Would you make your way over to the forensics lab?"

Tomlinson's face cracked into a grin. He was very fond of the obvious bond between Graham and his young protégé, and he shared the DI's high hopes for the keen young constable.

"That's right," Graham said. "I've got a task for you. There's a chap here called Simon Oxley. Tomorrow morning, get over to the lab and do everything he tells you. Right. Good lad." Graham ended the call.

"More manpower?" Tomlinson asked, his smile still in place.

"Something like that. Simon, I'm sending you an assistant. Teach him, put him to work, and get him to help you. You're going to figure out who wrote this letter and what it says," Graham said, turning to leave. "Most importantly, you're going to discover why we found it on the body of a dead man."

The man reached into his duffel bag and brought out one of the six 'burner' phones he'd brought to Jersey. He had hoped only to use one of them for the purpose of announcing the successful completion of his assignment, but three had already been used, shattered and discarded. Far from the quick, easy solution his employers sought, his time on the island had become unexpectedly complicated. Not to mention increasingly frustrating.

"What the *hell* do you mean?" the voice rasped on the other end.

The man had expected this anger and was relieved to be a couple of hundred miles away, rather than having to face this particular wrath in person. "Things got messed up by that old security guard dying on the job," he said. "There are cops all over the place."

"That was at the *museum*, if I recall," the voice continued, no less furious. "And your business is at the *library*, is it not?"

"Yeah," he admitted. "But there's been another complication. A murder."

"So?" came the exasperated voice.

The man sighed. "People are jumpy. Keeping their eyes open, you know? Some old bag across the road from the library called the cops three nights in a row."

The voice cut him off. "You know what I'm hearing? I'm hearing *excuses*. You have one job and one job only, and I don't want to hear from you again until it's done."

"No problem," the man replied instantly. "I got it covered, boss."

"Twenty-four hours. I want good news in *less* than twenty-four hours. Got it?"

"Leave it with me, boss," the man assured the voice on the end of the line. "I know exactly what to do."

CHAPTER TWENTY-FOUR

"WHERE THERE IS one," Graham noted, "there's the other." He regarded the two of them, Janice and Jack, working side by side behind the reception desk. "Sounds like a law firm, or something, doesn't it? Or maybe," he continued, "a firm of private detectives."

The younger pair looked up. "Huh?"

Graham mimed the sign across their imaginary storefront. "'Harding and Wentworth.' It's got a nice ring to it."

The couple blushed in tandem, a reaction Graham found endearing. "How was the forensics lab yesterday?" Harding asked. "Roach excited to be called down there at short notice?"

"I'm sure he was," Graham smiled, hanging up his jacket on the coat stand behind his office door and re-emerging in the reception area. "He's moving on from furniture analysis to graphology. What are you two finding?"

Jack shrugged. "I know it's my stock-in-trade to remind everyone that criminals can be unbelievably stupid, but this particular criminal has not yet fallen into that trap."

"Blast," Graham groaned. "I was hoping for just that kind of ineptitude. No sign of the medal, then?"

Wentworth shook his head. "Not yet, sir." Despite being an operative who stood outside the police chain of command, the fact that everyone else called DI Graham 'sir' had rubbed off on Jack. "He might be trying to sell it privately, of course. Probably more secure than flogging it online, especially if he has a buyer who doesn't care where it came from. Or he might have passed it on to a fence. But if he's after an anonymous quick return, the internet auction houses are the place to go. I'm trawling all possible outlets."

"I'll leave you to it, Jack. I need a cup of tea. Let me know if you find anything. Janice, come help me would you? It's making my head spin."

"The tea, sir?"

"This case, Sergeant."

Graham found his teapot and opened a tightly sealed metal container of Chinese jasmine. His ritual was comforting. Janice sat down in his office, noticing the unusually large pile of documents laid out on his desk. "Research, sir?"

"Yes," Graham replied, sighing at the mess. "That blessed Satterthwaite desk, among other things. The incidents involving Nobby Norris and Felipe Barrios have to be related, but how? We've got a guard who has a heart attack and dies, damaging a valuable desk on his way down, probably *during* a robbery. And a furniture restorer who is bludgeoned to death a few hours after receiving a phone call from an unidentified caller whilst working on said desk, and which we later find out had a hidden compartment that no one seemed to know about."

"Was anything in it?" Janice asked. "The compartment, I mean? I can't imagine having a hiding place as perfect as that and then not using it."

"Nothing in there when we opened it. But Tomlinson found a paper secreted in Barrios' jacket that they're attempting to decipher now. I sent Roach to help them. Tomlinson also found this photograph." He showed her the evidence bag with the curled up, faded Polaroid.

"Any idea who this might be, sir? In the photo? Or where it was taken?"

"None. You?" Janice shook her head.

Graham seemed to drift off, lost in thought, until a loud cheer broke out in the reception area. He was there in three seconds flat. "News?"

Jack was sitting back in his chair, triumphant. "I've got a hit on that medal."

Janice dashed around the side of the reception desk and read the screen. "Silly bugger thought we wouldn't notice. Does that make him brave or stupid?"

"Told you, didn't I?" Wentworth said, printing out the webpage. "Eight times out of ten, we catch them because they're impatient, greedy, or plain idiotic. This guy," he said, pointing to the screen, "takes detailed photos of a medal known to be missing following a burglary, and offers it for a pretty reasonable reserve price. He's looking for a quick sale, aiming at buyers who know what they're looking at and who understand its significance. Got his IP address and everything."

"Well, who is it?" Graham blurted out.

"Adam Harris-Watts," Harding said, looking up from searching the police database on her laptop.

Graham blinked. "Eh? You're *kidding* me."

"And," Wentworth added, "if you can believe this, he goes by the handle, 'Jersey Boy.' Remarkable, isn't it?"

Graham went around the desk to look at Janice's laptop, both relieved to have a suspect, and frustrated that he hadn't seen the connection earlier. "The little blighter burgled his own museum?"

"He's not breaking new ground, sir," Harding pointed out. "It's often staff who turn out to be light-fingered."

Graham growled under his breath. "Alright. Pick him up. Send Barnwell. That should give him a scare."

"Righto, boss," Harding said.

"Should make for an interesting conversation. And for you," Graham said to Wentworth, "dinner for two at the Bangkok Palace, on me."

"Thank you very much, sir." Wentworth smiled.

"Right. There's one little mystery solved. I'm going to check in with noted graphologist Constable Roach and see if he's close to giving us an answer about the rest of this maddening case."

Janice Harding bit into a much-needed egg and cress sandwich and watched Jack Wentworth pacing around the lobby of the police station as though waiting for news of his first born. "Does he usually take this long?" Jack asked.

"Barnwell? It depends. Most people come quietly once they realise the game is up. But there are always those who try to do a runner."

Jack stopped and imagined the scene. "And would he be able to... you know..."

Janice did smile this time. Quite enough jokes had already been made at the expense of her more rotund colleague, and Wentworth was too new to know the extraordinary and creditable journey Barnwell had already undertaken. "I would back him in a foot race against most any common criminal," she replied. "And he's a mean swimmer, if you remember. Brave, too."

Jack gave her an apologetic look. "I'm just impatient."

The sergeant set down her sandwich and settled further into the swivel chair behind the desk. "Exciting, isn't it?"

Just as Jack was nodding, Barnwell appeared at the door, towering over the diminutive figure of Adam Harris-Watts. "Sergeant Harding, I have some paperwork for you to do."

Janice began typing up the arrest record. "Ah, yes. I have to say, Mr. Harris-Watts, I'm sorry to see you like this."

Harris-Watts had very obviously been crying. He said nothing except to confirm his name and address, and that he understood his rights.

"Turn out your pockets, please," Janice told him. Harris-Watts emptied all the contents on to the desk as Janice catalogued them, noting that in addition to the usual wallet, phone, loose change, and used tissues, there were three plastic containers of green, white, and orange mints. "You need to go easy on those," she said. "Rot your teeth, they will."

Slumped and depressed, Harris-Watts was taken to a cell where he would await what Barnwell, Harding, and Wentworth all knew would be an intense grilling delivered by none other than Detective Inspector Graham.

Graham came out of his office. A crumpled paper on Barnwell's desk caught his eye as he passed. He twisted his head to look at it. "Is he here?" he mumbled.

"Barnwell just took him to the cells, sir. Do you want to interview him right away?"

"No, let's sweat him a bit first. What's this?" Graham waved the sheet of paper on Barnwell's desk that had attracted his attention.

"No idea, sir."

A banging of doors and heavy footsteps indicated Barnwell's arrival back in the office. Graham looked up. "Where did you get this?"

"That? Oh, some bloke dropped it in the coffee shop on the front. In a rush, he was. Thought I might see him as I biked around."

Graham looked down at it, reading. "What did he look like? Did you recognise him?

"No, sir. Tourist, I reckon. Heavyset guy. Late forties, early fifties. Why, sir? Something to do with a case?"

"Maybe, Constable. Keep an eye out for him. Ask around. If you see him again, bring him in."

Charlotte put down her cup of tea. She was watching the local lunchtime news on the television in her hotel room. Felipe Barrios was dead. Murdered. Charlotte's mind cast back to her conversation with Adam Harris-Watts, then to Don. Her eyes narrowed. She picked up her phone and dialled Don's number. "Don? It's me, Charlotte." This time there was no friendly banter. "Meet me at the castle at 3 p.m." She paused. "No, buts. Just be there." *Click.*

CHAPTER TWENTY-FIVE

DON TOOK THE steps quite slowly, hoping to avoid arriving on the castle's battlements out of breath. It had been another warm day. Once again, he found that he had arrived a few minutes in advance of Charlotte, and he enjoyed the colours cast by the sun over the Channel. He took in cleansing breaths of sea air, and paced along the ramparts to their far end, trying to relax.

"Good afternoon, sir," came a voice. "Beautiful view, isn't it?" Stephen Jeffries, Orgueil Castle's events manager strolled along the battlement's stone walkway toward Don.

"It is," Don said. The sea was taking on a yellow-green hue, the surface sparkling like stars in a spiritual universe. The two men met and stood side by side for a moment, admiring the view over the water.

"I work here almost every day but don't often stop to appreciate the simply *gorgeous* vista on my very doorstep," Jeffries explained. "I do apologise if I've interrupted your solitude," he said formally.

Don gave him a shrug. "I'm waiting for someone."

Jeffries beamed at him. "A romantic liaison? A proposal?" he speculated. "We do the most beautiful weddings, you know."

Don let out a short laugh. "No, most definitely not. Just some family business."

"Well," Jeffries said, straightening his waistcoat and tidying his hair, "I'll leave you to it. A nice spot for a quiet meeting, of whichever kind." He headed past Don with a nod and made his way down the spiral staircase back into the castle's interior, leaving Don alone in the sunshine. It was glorious, but not even the ethereal beauty of the mid afternoon sun on the sparkling surface of the water could calm Don's nervous, racing pulse.

"I'm starting to like it here," came a familiar, slightly haughty voice. Charlotte joined him on the battlements. "Not too windy, not too cold. A nice place for a picnic, maybe."

Don decided on a gruff, impatient demeanour. "Cut the chit-chat, Charlotte. I'm busy. What did you want me here for?"

She wore a no-nonsense trouser suit and heels that must have made the steps up to the ramparts something of a challenge. She walked toward him, her heels clacking on the stones beneath her. "Busy? That's good, Don. Keeping your mind occupied."

Don looked at her sideways. The memories of a whole decade of Charlotte's maddening, high-handed condescension when he was a teen welled up in Don's memory, but he bit down an angry rejoinder and simply waited for her to make her play.

"I asked you here because I think it important that we both know what the other is doing, don't you?" Charlotte said as she drew up close to him. "So, how *is* your investigation into the desk going?" she asked.

"That again! What *are* you on about? I don't *have* an investigation. I'm here for a break. I *told* you," Don answered.

Charlotte shook her head. "Really? No more trips down memory lane, following Mummy's tales of sorrow and strife? Come now, Don. Don't take me for a fool. Are you seriously expecting me to believe you are here merely on some kind of jolly? You're here to look for the letter, aren't you?"

He spotted the tell straight away. "So you *do* know about it."

Undeterred, Charlotte carried on. "And so, clearly, do you. How did you find out about it, hmm? Did mother dearest tell you? I've known about it for years. We used to look for it as kids but never found it. I'd prefer that it stay that way." Don stared at her. His nostrils flared.

Charlotte continued. "You want to find it so you can humiliate me and my family, don't you? You want your *revenge* for all those years your mother spent in the asylum. You want to destroy my career. Punishment for my father's 'misdeeds.'" Charlotte's eyes alternately flashed and narrowed as she cast out her accusations.

Don was shaking his head. "Perhaps, but I'll bet you want it even more. You're so desperate to make sure that you're the next Member of Parliament for Market Ellestry that you'll do *anything* to remove a potential threat."

"I'm a practical woman, it's true," she countered.

"And you know full well," Don continued, "that your father's reputation is already a bit... *muddy*, shall we say?"

"Nothing was ever proven," Charlotte said.

"Someone who would send away *his own wife* because she cried in despair once too often," Don growled.

"He did *everything* he could think of," Charlotte hissed.

"A penny-pinching tyrant? A tax-dodging tycoon? That's the man whose reputation you're so desperate to protect? Whose reputation could so badly affect your own?"

"Don't say those things! He was my father!" She spoke through gritted teeth. "He *loved* me!"

"Well, I wouldn't know what that felt like," Don shot back. "Tell me, Charlotte, last night you went to the workshop where the desk was being repaired and hit a man over the head didn't you? I heard about it on the news. Felipe Barrios. I knew it was you, straight away."

"I most certainly did not," his stepsister protested, coolly.

"And then," Don said, "you searched for the letter. But you didn't find it, did you? If you had, you'd be in Market Ellestry right now, keeping your head down and hoping the police don't decide to question you as part of their murder investigation."

"You've got a very active imagination."

Don paced in front of her, revelling in this chance to lecture his high-handed stepsister. "*This* is the kind of woman you are. And you're proposing to represent the good people of Market Ellestry? They need someone honest, not a scheming, selfish witch who throws murderous temper tantrums when she can't get her own way."

Charlotte cut across him. "You know what I think? I think it was you who broke in to that workshop and killed the repairer. Giving someone a quick bang on the head would be nothing to you if it meant you could avenge dear, sweet, old Mummy."

Near the top of the spiral staircase leading to the battlements, Stephen Jeffries listened. He had stepped aside on the stairs earlier to let Charlotte pass him. Now he found himself drawn to the ill-tempered sounds of a heated argument. Only yards away now, but hidden behind the thick castle walls, he listened to this brewing contretemps with genuine concern. "*Murder?*" he whispered to himself, reaching for his phone. "God... not again..."

On the ramparts, listening to Charlotte made Don's blood pressure soar. "Ha! You're so wrong. You thought *I* was the bumbling one. But *you're* the person who broke into a man's workshop and killed him. Which of us is the bumbler now?" he rasped, towering above her, his bulk giving menace to his accusations. "Which one of us," he roared, "is the *murderer?*"

Charlotte shrieked. Her hands lashed out. Fingernails caught the side of Don's face and raked his skin, leaving bloody scratches. "You're *nothing!*" she yelled, "But a lousy, lumpish loser."

Don recoiled but then seemed to remember the great heft of his own bulk. He came at her, sending her reeling back against the stone walls. "You're not going to push me around anymore," he roared defiantly.

Another harsh swipe of Charlotte's nails against his forehead drew more blood. She was like a panicked cat, claws protracted, searching for weakness. "You came here for revenge!" she countered. "But you've made everything worse. Just like always!"

Don stood menacingly in front of Charlotte, imprisoning her against the battlements with his sheer size. "What does it say, Charlotte?" he asked, his tone so much milder now. "The letter. The one he hid away in that beautiful old desk so secretly. What does it *say?*" His face was inches from hers.

Charlotte's palms were pressed flat against the stonework behind her. "I haven't," she said, her voice hoarse, "a bloody *clue*."

Don stood, his heart pumping hard, his fists balled, ready for combat. "You *must* know *something*," he insisted.

"I thought," Charlotte continued in the same pained tone, "that *you* knew. That's why you're here, isn't it? Because it's something scandalous? Something that would *ruin* me?"

Don shook his head and then took his step-sister by the shoulders with large, strong hands. "I've got upsetting news for you, Charlotte Hughes," he told her sternly. "You're not the centre of every bloody thing that happens in the world. I'm not *here* because of *you*."

Don spun her around, dragging Charlotte along the stonework toward a gap in the castle wall. Her heels scraped on the stones as she struggled, and Don forced her against the crenellations, designed centuries ago to protect Medieval archers, but now the scene of a desperate family struggle.

"Stop, you..." she complained, wriggling from his grip as her heels slipped on the stones. "Don..."

"Thomas Hughes was a *tyrant*," Don growled, "a liar, and a scoundrel. A bully and a crook. A heart attack was too good for him. He deserved a horrible death." He was pressing her against the battlements as though trying to force her body through them.

But Charlotte wasn't giving up. She felt the cold of the stone and the harshness of its unpolished surface against the back of her neck. "What about the guard at the museum, Don? Did he deserve to die, too?"

He lifted her now and found her so feather-light in his powerful grip that he could have tossed her up into the air and let the wind carry her out into the English Channel. "Did Felipe Barrios?" Don spat back at her. "Did he deserve to have his skull smashed in? Did..."

"Gorey Police! Stay where you are!" It was an authoritative voice, deep and commanding. "Put her down and step away." Barnwell filled the doorway at the top of the spiral staircase. Behind him cowered Stephen Jeffries.

Don froze. "Or what?" he demanded, reluctant to move.

"Let her go, sir," was the response, more calmly now as Barnwell inched his way along the battlements, his arm outstretched.

Don English stared at Charlotte. Her hair was messy in the wind, her lipstick smeared, her face ashen. It would have been so easy to manoeuvre her into the gap between the crenellations and simply push her away. But he found there, in Charlotte's face, just that victory he now realised had been his aim all along. The tables were turned, and her life was in his hands.

"Your father wasn't merciful," he told Charlotte in a hoarse whisper. "But I'm not a Hughes. My mother was an English, and I'm an English too." He let go of her shoulder. "And we don't treat people like this."

He dropped his hands from Charlotte's shoulders and turned to face the police officer, the wind and fury knocked out of him. "I'm sorry about this. I'm not a danger to anyone." Don looked back at Charlotte. "I think we'd better go with him," he said. "We both have a lot of explaining to do."

DI Graham stood and carried his cup of tea into the lobby. He watched as Barnwell brought in the pair. Charlotte stood defiantly. Don was meek, his shoulders slumped.

The constable left them with Harding and walked over to Graham. "Sir, this is the guy with the paper," he whispered quietly. Barnwell tossed his head over in Don's direction. "The one that dropped all his papers outside the coffee shop."

"Is that so?" Graham eyed the two standing at the custody desk. He thought for a moment.

"Are you going to interview them tonight, sir?" Barnwell asked.

"No, we'll put them in the cells. Let them stew."

"Thing is, sir, we don't have enough."

"Hmm?" Graham was still thinking.

"Cells, sir. We don't have enough for everyone."

Graham walked over to where Harding was registering the prisoners' details. He read over her shoulder. "Put Harris-Watts in the interview room for now, Sergeant. Mr. English can go in his cell. Ms. Hughes can go in the other."

"What about overnight, sir?"

"English and Harris-Watts can share if it comes to that." Graham smiled. "Let's hope it's not a typical Friday night, eh? Closing time could make things interesting in here."

The two old men left the library together, walking through the park near where the man was hiding. After they had passed, he crossed them both off his list of those he knew to be inside. "Empty," he sighed. "Finally."

It had been a long, frustrating day. The library closed late on Friday, but the last patrons had now gone, and Laura was tidying up the place on her own. It was the perfect moment, and one he had been waiting for all week.

He sent one last text on his burner phone: *All good. Target alone. Stand by.* He approached the library, checking his handgun with his fingertips inside his jacket pocket. Silencer on. Safety off. He climbed the few steps to the front entrance.

CHAPTER TWENTY-SIX

IT WASN'T THAT she minded working alone, but Laura found the dimmed, deserted library a little creepy once the sun began to go down. She had noticed the sensation several times during the past few days, that tingle in her skin that told her she was being watched. "Paranoia," she muttered to herself. *Calm down.* And yet, she could have sworn that she saw, or felt, a pair of eyes watching her from among the shelves. "Overactive imagination," she told herself. *Focus on your work.*

Laura had been locking the cabinets behind the large, open tabletop of the distribution desk, and it was when she straightened up that she first saw the looming figure at the library's locked door. With most of the building's interior lights now switched off as part of the evening routine, and with the sun already set behind the row of homes opposite the front door, it was hard to see who this late visitor might be.

Laura smiled as she opened the door slightly. It was a library patron she thought, though not one she recognised.

"We're finished for the day, I'm afraid," she told the man. He was big, perhaps fifty and dressed in a leather jacket.

"Oh, I won't stay long, I promise," he said.

Laura's immediate sense was that his lilting, sing-song accent, which was hard to place, was not truly his own. "We open tomorrow at nine," she told him and made to close the door.

A large foot jammed itself quickly into the remaining space, and she felt the door shoved powerfully open, sending her tipping back onto the floor of the library's lobby. "Please!" she gasped. "There's no money here."

The man closed the door behind him, and stood over the terrified Laura. One hand was in his jacket pocket, and she knew that it would soon emerge with a weapon. "I'm not here for money," the man told her. "I'm here to shut you up for good."

Laura tried to scramble to her feet, but the man's boot was on her ankle, hard and insistent, painfully pinning her down. "No!" she yelled putting her hand up, the other propping her upper body off the floor. "I promise I won't say another word. I won't testify. I... I won't go back there. Not *ever*."

The man's hidden hand emerged, and Laura watched him bring back the action of a small, silver pistol. He did it steadily, as though relishing the occasion. "No, you won't," he assured her. "There won't be no trial, and there won't be no wit—. *Arggh*."

A hardback volume of poetry flew through the air, sharp and direct and seemingly out of nowhere. It struck the man hard on the shoulder. He slipped on the tiled floor. Laura's ankle released, she bolted for the distribution desk, seeking cover behind its reassuring bulk.

"What the..." Another volume of poetry arrived, even

before the man could complete the curse. It beat against his chest, and then another sailed over his shoulder. This one narrowly avoided hitting him on the side of the head, causing him to duck. "Who's there?" he bellowed. "Come out here!"

The answer was another airborne book that bounced harmlessly onto the floor by the man's feet, and then a flurry of quick footsteps. "Damn you!" He levelled the pistol but saw no one, hearing only the sound of running feet as they receded into the space around the shelves in the main part of the library. The man turned. He had no time for flying books. He needed to finish this job. But Laura was gone.

He swore loudly and colourfully at the ceiling of the library. His only clues were the faint footsteps, now two pairs rather than one. They told him that Laura had disappeared into the gloomy depths of the library, and that her erstwhile saviour had done likewise. He unleashed one more powerful oath and stomped toward the rows of eight-foot tall shelves. They lay in chevrons, one behind the other, flanking the central reading space with its tables and magazine racks. As he looked around for a light switch, he heard more shuffling and dashing of footsteps. He swore again as the sounds carried down the corridors between the bookcases.

In the gloom, Laura ducked down behind the shelves. They would shield her from the man's view. She had just caught her breath when she heard faint skittering sounds and, before she could even turn, someone appeared beside her, panting as quietly as he could.

"Billy?" Laura whispered. "Oh, Billy for heaven's sake!"

"Are you okay?" he asked. "He didn't hurt you?"

Laura placed her hand on the boy's head. His hair was

matted with sweat, but he was unharmed. "No, but he won't stop until he does."

Pistol drawn, the man paced down each row of shelving, stopping to peer between books. At the end of the third row of shelves, he turned to check whether Laura had doubled back toward the distribution desk. Suddenly, out of nowhere, another heavy volume hit him right in the face. His gun went off, shattering a floor tile. The sounds of the debris skittering across the space were louder than the retort of the silenced shot. In the relative silence that followed, he was certain that he heard the voice of a child.

Roach kept his grip on the phone deliberately strong, as he risked dropping it out of sheer surprise. He was hissing into it as Barnwell told him of the day's events. "You're *kidding* me, right, Barnwell? You're pulling my leg. I get seconded for a day and *this* happens. Three arrests? You're a superstar."

"It was a bit of a madhouse in there for a while, mate." Barnwell puffed and paused as he went down a gear and dug in to pedal his way up the hill away from the front. "What're you doin' in the station, anyway?"

"Dropped in to pick up my football cleats. Janice asked me to take the phones whilst she pops out to get a takeaway for the guv." Roach opened his mouth to ask more about the day's arrests, but stopped himself. "Gotta go. Red phone."

"Okay, Roachie. Call me if you need anything."

Roach skidded around the corner of his desk and grabbed the red handset. "Gorey Police." He listened for a moment and took notes. Four seconds into the call, his pen paused on his notepad. He abruptly moved over to the radio transmitter.

"Mike Bravo 882, are you receiving? Over."

"Mike Bravo 882 receiving loud and clear. Over," Barnwell responded.

"Report of active shooter situation at Gorey Library."

"Yeah, right, son. Nice one, Roachie."

"No, that's the report, Bazza…"

"Says who?"

"Mrs. Hollingsworth, the little old lady that keeps reporting suspicious strangers in the area."

Barnwell sighed wearily. He braked to a stop and turned his bike around. "Okay, well, roger that, dispatch. ETA three minutes. Don't hold your breath."

"Keep the line open, 882."

CHAPTER TWENTY-SEVEN

"OVER HERE!" THE man followed the child's voice but found the whole area behind the shelves empty. It was like chasing smoke, he grumbled to himself as he hauled his generous frame around the spacious building. "Come out, wherever you are!" he called. "You can't escape!"

Another book came flying at him. This time, with a fraction of a second to spare, he caught sight of Billy before the boy ducked down behind one of the desks in the centre of the library. "Didn't your mother teach you to treat books nicely?" the man muttered, levelling his weapon at the table. His quarry would break either left, toward the Recommended Reading table, or right, toward the New Acquisitions display. Either way, he would be exposed for a moment. The man would be ready.

"Over here, you fat gibbon!" Billy's high voice penetrated the murkiness of the library.

The man whirled around and caught sight of Laura standing in the open, just by the distribution desk. He loosed off a wild round and then another as he steadied the gun, training it on the desk area. But Laura was gone again, apparently as nimble as the kid. He cursed yet again. He turned to see the boy sprinting down one of the rows of shelving to his left. "Not so fat," he shouted back, "that I can't chase you around all night, if that's what it takes!" The boy disappeared around the end of the book shelves.

Then he heard it again, from over his shoulder. It came from the other side. Laura now, drawing out the insult like a boxing announcer. "Fat gibbon!" But still, he couldn't see her. He spun around, tracing the source of the sound, but all he heard were footsteps.

The man fired his pistol at the ceiling twice, and then roared in deafening anger. For a man of his size, he could move pretty fast, but he began to realise that he would never catch Billy, or Laura for that matter, in a footrace. They were constantly wrong footing him, their deeper knowledge of the library outwitting him. He sagged down onto his knees near the distribution desk, catching his breath and taking a moment to check his weapon. Six rounds fired, all needlessly, and only three left. He shrugged off his heavy leather jacket and rose to one knee, still panting hard. "Bloody kid," he muttered.

Billy found Laura on the opposite side of the library, almost as far from the wheezing man as she could be. "We need to escape!" he hissed. "I could…"

Laura ruffled his hair. "No more book-throwing, Billy. Someone will have called the police by now. They'll be here soon, and this will all be over."

"Yes, but…"

"Let's watch him carefully. If, *if* we get a chance, we'll

run for the doors." She was being brave for Billy's sake. In truth, her heart was pumping with fear, and there was a strange tingle in her fingertips. She desperately hoped that what she'd told Billy was true, that the police were on their way. She was much too frightened to call them herself.

They both watched the man stumble into the centre of the room and begin yet another sweep of the shelves to his left and right. He was too slow, too lumbering, and too unwilling to head down each row to see if they were hiding at the very far corner. He reached the end of the row of shelves, as far from the lobby as he'd ventured.

"Now, Billy!" They ran behind the man and toward the distribution desk and the front door.

The man caught their movements but turned too slowly. He let off a round which exploded through a hard-bound volume of the *Encyclopaedia Britannica,* throwing up a cloud of paper confetti. Another shot thunked into the wood of the distribution desk. He dashed forward and closed the distance between himself and the pair. Billy opened the library door and ran through it. He ran into the car park passing a large, burly police officer coming the other way, baton out and speaking quickly into his lapel radio.

The policeman barged into the library, obstructing Laura's escape. Her assailant grabbed her and pulled her back further inside the library, pressing her body against his and ramming his gun into her neck, his eyes defiant in the face of the bobby's bulk.

Barnwell cursed. He threw himself across the floor, sliding on his hip. He took cover behind the distribution desk. He was armed only with his baton and a canister of CS spray, which would be of no use over distance. "Gorey

Police!" he shouted from behind the desk. "Let's stay calm now, alright?"

There was a low, cynical chuckle from the gunman. "Oh, dear," he chided, "You've gone and wandered into the middle of somethin', haven't you? You forget, I've got the girl. And the gun."

Barnwell rose to one knee. "Gorey Police!" he repeated. "There's no need for anyone to get hurt. Set down your weapon, and show me your hands."

Another chuckle resonated around the library, longer than before. "You think I'll come quietly, eh, copper?" the man shouted. Laura gasped and shuddered against his body.

Barnwell tracked their sounds. The gunman was forcing Laura past the reading desks and toward the library door. The officer drew his CS spray and began shuffling, as quietly as he could, along the length of the distribution desk, and toward the corner. There he would wait. He couldn't risk rounding the edge of it.

"We can work this out," Barnwell shouted back. "How this ends is entirely up to you." The man laughed. "Let her go," Barnwell urged.

"Let her go? She's my 'get out of jail free' card," the gunman laughed again. He was still walking forward. Barnwell could hear footsteps, and the man's ragged breath. "I want out of here," the gunman shouted to him. "A car. No funny business, or there'll be more corpses to read about in the papers." As the pair moved forward, Barnwell rounded the corner and slid along the short end of the distribution desk that was now behind them.

In an instant, the man threw Laura sprawling to the floor and bolted for the door. Barnwell set off like a sprinter, CS spray in his left hand, baton in his right. The man began to turn, gun poised, and for a second their eyes locked like bulls in a fight. Barnwell launched himself, grabbing the man around the hips and toppling him with a rugby tackle that would distinguish a professional. The two fell to the floor. Barnwell unleashed the CS spray six times into the man's face. The gunman gurgled and roared and spat at him, but he didn't fire. A moment later, the gunman, his eyes streaming and nausea welling in his gut, found his hands cuffed behind him.

"You're a big, strong lad," Barnwell said, puffing only slightly as he stood up, "to be chasing a woman and a boy around a library, at night, with a gun." Then he spoke into his lapel radio. "Mike Bravo 882 to Gorey. Active shooter situation contained. Suspect in custody. One juvenile, one female in need of medical assistance for shock. Firearms team were a little slow, but everything's under control. Over."

The reply was a decidedly non-regulation stream of congratulatory utterances from Constable Roach, followed by, "Hold tight. Transport on its way."

CHAPTER TWENTY-EIGHT

"NO LAWYER, MR. Harris-Watts?" Graham asked as he took his seat. "Do you think that's wise, sir?"

Harris-Watts was shattered. He had cried throughout the hours he had spent in his cell, and he periodically broke down again whenever anyone spoke to him, even if it was to ask if he would like a cup of tea. "I was... I was going to plead guilty. I didn't think I'd need... You know... With the cost, and everything."

Graham sat back and folded his arms. "Plead guilty to *what*, exactly?"

Harris-Watts blinked repeatedly. He rubbed his eyes with his knuckles. "The medal. You know. On the morning we found Nobby. I pinched it. I admit it," he sniffed.

"Ah, yes, the medal," Graham said. "I'm glad you've cleared that up for us." Harris-Watts stared at the table in utter hopelessness.

"Tell me all of it," Graham ordered. "Everything about what happened when you went to the museum on Monday morning."

Harris-Watts visibly fought with himself to look at the DI. "Okay," he said, sniffing. He was rubbing his hands on his thighs, rocking back and forth, visibly trying to bring himself under control. "Okay. I went into work and found Nobby on the floor and glass everywhere. I called nine-nine-nine, and then checked for a pulse, but he was so cold, I knew he was gone." He shivered at the memory. "Then, I checked to see if anything was missing. Nothing appeared to be, so I went to my office and checked the CCTV. With the images being so poor, I knew you wouldn't be able to pin the break-in on anyone." He looked Graham in the eye, more confident now he was confessing. "I've got debts, you see," he admitted. "I've got expensive tastes. Too expensive for my salary. So, I forced open the medal case, instead of smashing it, you know, so it would look professional. I took one that I knew was valuable."

Graham listened, arms folded. "Go on."

"I put it on an underground auction site I sometimes look at, just out of curiosity, and someone bid on it. I thought I'd made thousands, and that no one would ever know. Then your constable came to my house and arrested me."

"And?" Graham pressed.

Harris-Watts shrugged, blinking. "That's it. Now, I'm here. It's the first time I've been in a prison cell in my life. Will I... Will I go to... to *jail* for this?"

Graham closed the door. He took several slow, deep breaths —a practice he called his "Buddha Moment." They were a way for him to bring a greater clarity to the present and help set aside the often fruitless hours of accusations and counter defences he waded through and was a part of. As he stood there, inhaling deep, slow breaths, he tried to unravel the strange conundrum this case had become. Calmer, the DI approached the desk, where Roach and Harding were listening to the police frequency on the radio. "What's going on?" he asked.

"There's been an active shooter situation at the library, sir," Harding replied.

"WHAT?" Graham stood still, wide-eyed, thoughts careering around his brain like a cascade of shooting stars hurtling around a galaxy.

Harding set down the earphones and smiled. "The situation has been resolved, sir," she said. "All is well. It was very quick. The hostages, the new librarian and Billy Foster, are safe and being checked out by the paramedics. The shooter is in custody. The suspect was apprehended thanks to the heroics of a certain Constable Barnwell. The press'll be here soon, I'll bet. Probably be another glowing article in the paper."

"But... But why didn't you inform me?" Graham was staring at her. He appeared stunned.

"Erm, well sir, we didn't really believe it, see?" Roach said, looking sheepish. "We, Barnwell and I, just thought it was old Mrs. Hollingsworth imagining things again. Seems we got it wrong, sir. Sorry, sir."

"Sorry? An apology is hardly sufficient, Constable! This could have turned into a complete, unmitigated disaster." Graham's voice was hard now. "I can see that we shall have to put some serious effort into more training later in the year." Roach looked at Janice who looked down at her feet.

"Yes, sir," Roach whispered.

Graham glared at them momentarily, then collected himself and thumped the desk, gently. "Barnwell again, eh?

That's the third time he's been the hero of the hour in recent months. He's in danger of making it a habit."

"He's bringing the shooter in now, sir," Roach said, talking quickly.

"Where are you going to put him?" Graham asked.

Roach smiled. "We've called St. Helier, and they're sending a firearms unit to meet the prisoner here. They'll handle him. Should be here any minute."

Graham marvelled at how far his small, formerly raggle-taggle team had come in a few short months, even if there was still some way to go.

"I'll leave you to it, Sergeant, Constable. But do come and find me if there's a terrorist incident on our patch, won't you?" He turned. "I'm all done with Mr. Harris-Watts. Would you be so good as to take him back to his cell?"

"Yes, sir." Harding was looking at him curiously.

"Good." Graham shifted again. "You're quite sure that no one was hurt?"

"Quite sure, sir."

"Well, then. Jolly good... Carry on, Sergeant."

CHAPTER TWENTY-NINE

IT WAS A bright, cold Saturday morning. Don English sat in his cell quietly. He was in whispered consultation with his lawyer as Charlotte was with hers. Unsurprisingly, Charlotte had called Carl Prendergast within moments of arriving at Gorey police station. When he finally arrived, Prendergast exuded the air of someone very reluctant indeed. Don was offered, and accepted, the court-appointed duty solicitor on call.

"Ready, Sergeant?" Graham asked, setting down his teacup. "I say we start with Charlotte Hughes."

Harding and Graham exchanged a look as they stood at the interview room door. "Is this a case of 'watch and learn,' sir?" Harding asked. "Or do you want me to…"

"Let's see how we get on. You remember the signal?"

Harding nodded, and Graham gave her an encouraging smile as he pushed open the door to the interview room. "Good morning, Ms. Hughes," he said. He took a seat. Harding sat next to him, opposite Charlotte and Prendergast at the small interview room's table. "It's been quite a few days for you, hasn't it?" Graham said.

Prendergast laid out the formalities. "My client has decided to exercise her right to silence," he said in his clipped, formal tone. He was short, balding, and somewhere in his mid-sixties. Graham felt he might make a good King Lear or an officious bureaucrat in a period TV drama. There was something about his manner—superior, a bit blustery and bombastic—which made Graham dislike him immediately. Although it was his legal obligation to let the lawyer speak, and for his comments to be entered into the taped record, Graham ignored almost everything Prendergast said.

"As you already know, you've been arrested in connection with the murder of Felipe Barrios," Graham said, scanning Charlotte's face for signs of a reaction. All he saw was a pale, wan visage that signalled exhaustion.

"And when forensic evidence of the crime is presented to us," Prendergast retorted in his testy, nasal tone, "we will understand quite why that is so."

"All in good time," Graham told him.

Prendergast looked at Charlotte, hoping for some kind of sign. She was absolutely white, drained of fight and spark, defeated in a way Graham found almost pitiable. She wore a blue, hooded sweatshirt and trousers that Janice had found for her the evening before as they bagged her clothes for forensic examination. Her designer blouse had been torn beyond repair during the bitter exchanges on the battlements.

"You live on the mainland, Ms. Hughes, is that right?"

"Yes, in Market Ellestry. I am, *was*, hoping to become their Member of Parliament at the next election. Doubt that will happen now," Charlotte said, a hint of bitterness creeping into her tone.

"And what are you doing on Jersey? The elections aren't

that far away. Shouldn't you be in your constituency? Knocking on doors? Pressing the flesh?" Graham was being droll. He didn't have much time for politicians. Carl Prendergast leant forward and opened his mouth to interrupt.

"Shut up, Carl!" Charlotte's mouth curled as she said the words. Her arms were folded. She turned her head away from her legal counsel and stared down at her lap.

"I came here to arrange for repairs to my father's desk."

"I see. Is that all? Couldn't that be done over the phone?"

Charlotte coughed several times to clear her throat. "I was concerned... About the break-in at the museum and the damage to the desk." Graham lifted his chin and waited. Charlotte looked at him, eventually sighing. "And, well if you must know, that Don was missing after speaking to Carl about the desk in the hours before the break-in. I thought he might be up to something."

Graham stared at Prendergast. "You spoke to Don English about the desk?"

"Yes," Prendergast said. "Is that a crime?"

"Yes! It makes you a witness! You cannot be representing Ms. Hughes if you're a witness. Get out of here! Harding, take Mr. Prendergast and keep him in reception. If he gives you any trouble, arrest him. Jesus, man."

Prendergast didn't need to be told twice. He scuttled out of the room.

"Ms. Hughes, do you want to call the duty solicitor before we continue?"

Charlotte sighed, wearily. "No, no. Let's get this over with." She leant her forearms on the table and faced Graham across it. She seemed more at ease now that Prendergast was out of the room. "I thought Don might be here on Jersey looking for something. Something I really didn't want found, something that could damage my bid for election. I wanted to find out what he knew, if he'd found it."

"And what was that 'something' pray?"

"A letter," she croaked. "I've never known what it said. But I knew it would be damaging to my family."

"And does your brother have it?"

"*Step*brother," Charlotte murmured. "No. Yes. Oh, I don't know. I tried to flush him out, but well, you know what happened at the castle. He just flipped. Crazy. He wants to ruin me, and with a temper like his, who knows what he's capable of?"

"What do you know of the repairs that were being completed on your father's desk?"

"I know the cost of them and the name of the person making the repairs. I also know that he was killed.

"And do you know anything about that? About the killing of Felipe Barrios?"

Charlotte looked Graham squarely in the eyes. She stared into them for a full three seconds before replying. "Absolutely not."

CHAPTER THIRTY

GRAHAM SPIED BARNWELL at the reception desk. "Come with me, Constable. Harding can cover. We've got some investigating to do."

Ten minutes later, they pulled up at Don English's B&B at the same time. Barnwell propped his bike against the front garden railings. Graham found a parking spot just two doors down. He strolled along the pavement to join the constable outside the gate.

"I'm impressed with your commitment, Barnwell. Would never have had you down as a cycling man."

"Does me good, sir. The fresh air and the exercise."

The sun was shining directly onto the small terraced house, the glare from the upstairs window forcing them to shield their eyes. Barnwell pressed the catch of the wrought iron gate with a "ting," and they walked silently up to the front door. Blue and purple hyacinths in pots on either side emitted a delightful aroma as they waited for Don's landlady. They held their police IDs at the ready to reassure her.

"Yes?" Mrs. Lampard said as soon as she opened the door. She was well into her seventies and tiny. She peered up at the two men through horn-rimmed glasses. Graham reckoned that he towered over her by at least a foot.

"We're from Gorey Constabulary, ma'am. I rang earlier. About your guest, Mr. English? We'd like to see his room."

"Oh yes, come on in," Mrs. Lampard stood back to let them through. I'm glad to have caught you, I'm just back from the hairdresser's." She gently patted her cotton candy spun hair. There was a faint purple hue to it.

"How is business at this time of year, Mrs. Lampard?"

"It's a bit slow right now, but starting the end of next month, I'll be full until September. It's always like that, like clockwork." Mrs. Lampard held onto the bannister rail. She looked as though she could barely make a cup of tea, let alone a bed and a full English breakfast on a daily basis.

"When was the last time you had a booking? Before Mr. English."

"Couple of weeks ago. God willing, I'll have another before high season starts. My pension doesn't go very far these days."

"If you'd be so kind as to show us Mr. English's room....?"

"First on the left at the top of the stairs," she said, unnecessarily indicating the flight of stairs that loomed ahead of them. The two men trotted up as she watched.

The room was sunny and decorated brightly. Yellow daffodils sat in a fussy blue vase on a chest of drawers. Next to it, there was a tray with tea-making paraphernalia and a plastic kettle. In the corner was a small, white ceramic sink. Beside the taps sat soap, a face cloth, and shaving equipment. There was a toothbrush sticking out of a glass.

Graham looked around, mentally cataloguing everything he saw. The bed had been made. Don's old-fashioned, striped pyjamas were folded and neatly placed on the pillow. A battered paperback sat on the bedside table. In the corner was a wicker laundry basket that had seen better days. Several of the willow twigs had escaped their confines and splayed out waiting to injure the next person who came close. On a table under the window were papers neatly stacked.

"What are we looking for, sir?" Barnwell asked as Graham handed him a pair of latex gloves.

"Anything, Constable, anything that could tie Don English to the break-in at the museum or the Barrios' murder. Here, bag the toothbrush for DNA." Graham held out an evidence bag. "And go take a look in the bathroom." Barnwell picked the toothbrush out of the cloudy glass and dropped it into the bag before disappearing down the hallway to the bathroom Don had shared with his host.

Graham wandered over to the window. After giving the papers that lay on the table underneath it a cursory look, he started opening drawers in the chest next to it. There was nothing in them. Don clearly hadn't settled himself in, and so Graham moved to the open suitcase that lay on the floor. It was a jumble of clothes and belongings.

"Nothing in there, sir," Barnwell said coming back in the room. "Find anything?"

Graham stood up from the suitcase. "Nothing in this case, that's for sure. Take a look at those papers on the table by the window. Do they look like the notes that Don English dropped in the café?"

Barnwell looked them over without touching them. "Yup, I'd say. 'LETTER,' 'DESK,' 'MYSTERY PERSON.' Looks pretty incriminating, sir."

Graham moved over to the tall, imposing oak wardrobe in the corner of the room and turned the key that sat in the lock. The door swung open immediately, creaking. There on the bottom shelf was a gun. Graham picked it up carefully. He knew immediately it was a fake. It wasn't nearly heavy enough to be real. He held it up to the light.

"Cowboys and indians, sir?" Barnwell asked.

"Cowboys certainly, son." Graham bagged it and set it down next to the piles of paper. "Check under the bed, would you?" Graham moved over to the bedside table, opening the drawer and flipping through the pages of the dusty Bible that he found inside.

"Sir?"

"Hmm?"

"There's something here, sir," Barnwell was lying on his front, his arm outstretched as he strained to reach under the double bed. Carefully he dragged out an object wrapped in a cloth. Barnwell sniffed.

"It smells of something, sir. Can't place it, though." Graham came over.

"Varnish, Constable. Well, come on. Open it up!"

Barnwell gingerly opened the cloth. His eyes widened. "Got him, sir!" Wrapped inside was a thin round metal file about ten inches long.

"Would you boys like a cup of tea?" The two men turned, surprised by Mrs. Lampard's voice.

"Oh no, thank you. We'll be done shortly," Graham said, disappointing Barnwell who could have murdered a cup.

"Did you find anything? This is my room normally. I can make more money from it than the spare room. Is Mr. English in any trouble? I do hope not."

"Just routine, ma'am," Graham said.

"Not for me, Inspector, not for me. It's quite exciting, isn't it? Are you sure you don't want a cup of tea?"

"Quite sure, thank you. But you can put the kettle on, if you'd like."

"Oh, why's that?"

"Because this room is going to be crawling with a crowd of scenes of crime officers very shortly, and I'm sure they'd like a cuppa when they're done."

CHAPTER THIRTY-ONE

"OH GOOD," DON breathed as Graham came into the interview room. "I'm so glad you're here."

Graham glared at him as he sat down opposite. "That's not a reaction I get very often," he said. In contrast to Carl Prendergast, Don's solicitor sat quietly, taking notes.

Don shrugged. "I think I'll be the least complicated part of this whole business," he said. He held his hands up. "I confess."

"Really?" Graham opened his notebook in a response conditioned by years of interviews. He began to write.

Don put his elbows on the table and rubbed his face with his hands. When he pulled them away, he sighed and said, "I broke into the museum last Sunday night. I was looking for a hidden compartment inside the Satterthwaite desk, but I didn't get very far."

"You were interrupted by someone?" Graham asked.

"The guard. We said a few things to each other. Threats and such," Don said. "He was in the middle of backing off when he just went down like a sack of spuds."

Graham kept writing. "He had a name, Mr. English. Nobby Norris. He'd been working as a security guard at the museum for three years. He enjoyed football and a pint down the pub."

"Yes, sorry. I feel terrible about his death. I'm so sorry."

"And so Mr. Norris collapsed, did he? Right in front of you?"

Don mimed the event with his hands. "*Thump.* I figured he'd just lost his balance, or fainted for a moment."

"You didn't think to come to his aid?"

"I expected him to get right up and chase me out of there! I was so scared that I legged it back out through the window."

"But he didn't get up, did he?"

"I didn't know that!" Don insisted. "It was dark in there, and I couldn't see what had happened to him. Not properly. I'm not an experienced criminal, you know. Never even stolen a pack of gum from the corner shop."

"A man died, Mr. English. He left behind a widow, two sons, and three grandchildren. I doubt they care two hoots about the status of your criminal record at this point. You threatened him with *a gun*! The fact is he may still be alive today if you hadn't broken into the museum and scared him to death."

"Yes, yes, Detective. You're right. I feel terrible, but I didn't *mean* it to happen. If I could turn the clock back, I would. I simply wanted to see inside the desk." Don appealed, his palms up. "I think it better to own up to what I've done and let justice take its course. It was utterly stupid of me, and I won't ever forget it. I'm sorry. I know I need to pay."

Graham sighed and set aside his notebook. "The thing is, Mr. Norris's death notwithstanding, you're in a pile of other trouble, aren't you?" Don looked at him blankly. Graham waited for him to speak, but when nothing was forthcoming, he continued. "That desk you were so keen to check out. The person repairing it, Felipe Barrios, he was murdered." Graham noticed small beads of sweat had appeared on English's brow.

"Yes, I know. I heard about it on the news. Terrible."

"So what do you know about that?"

"Nothing." English shook his head.

Graham looked at him carefully. "Nothing? Okay, talk to me about your room at the B&B you're staying at."

Don pursed his lips and shook his head slowly from side to side. "It's just a B&B. I checked in on Sunday. The landlady is pleasant enough. Good breakfasts. Why?"

Graham bent to look at the notes in front of him. "What about the object we found under your bed?" He looked up at Don, sceptically.

Don stared at him. "What kind of object?"

"A file."

"A file?" Don said. "You mean, like papers?"

"A metal file," Graham said.

Don raised his eyebrows and shoulders simultaneously. He gave a sheepish grin. "Oh, I don't know anything about that. I don't do DIY." There was a confused look on his face.

"I don't suppose you do murder, either," Graham said quietly. "Maybe just dabble in it now and again when you're feeling like it, hmm?" He placed both hands on the table. "We have reason to believe the file we found under your bed was used to murder Mr. Barrios."

Don lurched up and to the right, startled into a spasm of panic. "Mur... Murder?" he gasped. "But, I..."

"The file was wrapped in a cloth that we have good

reason to believe came from the victim's workshop. Will we find your DNA on it, Don?"

Shaking, muttering, then trying to stand, Don was a miserable sight. "No," he said, over and over. "No, that's wrong, that's wrong, that's wrong. No, no, no, no, noooooo!"

Graham ignored Don's dramatic display. It was just this kind of questioning that brought suspects to those points of extremis and panic where the truth would emerge. "Where were you the night Barrios was killed?"

"In bed, of course. At my B&B."

"Can anyone vouch for you?"

"My landlady doesn't like people coming and going, and I've been respecting her wishes. She could confirm it."

"Do you have a key?"

"Yes, but—"

"Hardly a cast iron alibi then, is it Mr. English?"

Don said nothing. There was a knock on the door. It was Harding. "It's Tomlinson," she said, handing Graham a phone when they were outside the room.

Graham tapped the mute button. "Marcus? Are you going to make my day even more extraordinary?"

"Results on the file, old chap. It was definitely the murder weapon. Plenty of Barrios' DNA on it, but no prints or anything to connect it to Don English. Or anyone else for that matter."

"Damn! What about the cloth? Did that come from the workshop?"

"The chemical composition of the varnish on the cloth matched that found in a can on the workbench next to the desk, so I think we can be pretty sure on that. The strange thing is, there's a hair caught up in the threads of the cloth. Isn't a match for anyone. Not Barrios, his wife, Charlotte Hughes, or English. It's an odd colour, a sort of lavender."

"Probably the landlady's. She has a purple tint to her hair. I'll send someone to get a DNA sample from her. Anything else?"

"No, nothing, sorry." Tomlinson rang off. Graham blew out his cheeks and looked up at the ceiling.

CHAPTER THIRTY-TWO

GRAHAM GAVE THE departing van a quick salute. "Farewell, Adam Harris-Watts. Until your trial, anyway." Charged with three different offences relating to the theft of the medal, Graham expected Harris-Watts to be bailed and required to wear an electronic tag until his trial.

The detective inspector strode back through the reception area. For Janice and Jack's benefit, Barnwell was re-enacting his rugby tackle of Frank Bertolli, whose arrest was causing quite a flutter at Scotland Yard.

"He's wanted in connection with *six* gang-related murders," Harding told Graham.

"Yes, but what the *hell* was he doing on Jersey?" Graham asked. "And at the *library*, for heaven's sake?" Harding gave him a look that he found hard to interpret.

Barnwell moved on to the find of the morning. "Then at the B&B, there was all kinds of notes about the desk and such. Even a cloth that smells of varnish. Couldn't be more obvious. A metal file, about ten inches long. We sent forensics down there, pronto."

"Don't count your chickens. The metal file was definitely the murder weapon, but SOCO hasn't turned up anything to connect us to a murderer yet," Graham said on his way to his office. "Barnwell, I need you to get a DNA sample from Mrs. Lampard. We need to rule her out."

Graham's interview with English and his conversation with Tomlinson had left him puzzled. He'd pushed, and Don had wilted. He'd pressed, and Don had looked ready to fold. But the bedevilled man hadn't actually *admitted* anything. Without DNA evidence to connect Don to the crime or a confession, Graham was looking at highly circumstantial evidence at best. That wasn't good enough.

"I'm going to take another run at Charlotte Hughes, Janice. Can you bring her to the interview room?"

"Before you do that, sir," Janice said, trotting alongside him. "Jack has found something interesting." She showed Graham Felipe Barrios' phone records. "Remember he received a call in the evening before he was murdered? We can't trace it. Must have come from a burner."

"Tell him to keep at it, Harding,"

"He also found something else." Janice's tone stopped Graham now. He listened carefully.

"The number comes up again. This time on the records of a completely different phone."

"Whose?"

"Charlotte Hughes. Charlotte Hughes and Felipe Barrios both received a call from the same untraceable number the night he died."

🌍

Graham sat opposite Charlotte. He was tired. It had been a long day. "Felipe Barrios received a call on the night of his death. Prior to that call being made, you also received one from the same number. Is there anything you'd like to say about that, Ms. Hughes?"

Charlotte sat back abruptly in her seat. She turned down the corners of her mouth and shook her head. "No. Who is this call supposed to be from? I receive a lot of calls." She shrugged.

"I was hoping you'd tell me."

Charlotte flushed. She looked about her, drawing her breath in one long inhale.

"Is there something you're not telling me, Ms. Hughes?" Charlotte looked up at the ceiling, her hands clasped across her body. Her thumbs were tapping her sides furiously. "Because if there is, and you're not," Graham continued, "I could have you bang to rights on so many charges, your dreams of a future, let alone a parliamentary career, would be but a puff of smoke." He leant in toward Charlotte, who glared at him.

"I don't know anything that's relevant." Charlotte responded.

"Let me decide what's relevant." Graham waited. He didn't take his eyes off the woman across the table. Charlotte looked away.

"Look, I..." She sighed. "I wanted to flush out if Felipe Barrios had the letter by offering to buy it. But it didn't go anywhere. Barrios wouldn't sell or didn't have it. I don't know which," she added quickly.

"You called him?"

"No, I couldn't risk it." Charlotte took a deep breath, as she seemed to find some resolve. "No, I wasn't *brave* enough to make the call myself." She looked back at Graham.

"Then who did?"

"I asked my campaign manager, Lillian Hart, to do it

for me."

"Where is this Lillian Hart now?"

"At home, I assume. Miles away. In Market Ellestry."

"Are you sure?"

Charlotte stared at him, "Well, no actually. I haven't spoken to her since I asked her to make the call to Barrios."

"And when was that?"

"Tuesday. Tuesday evening."

Graham frowned. "What does she look like?"

"Oh, I don't know. Late fifties, five foot ten, large build. Likes bright loud clothes, lots of makeup. Smokes like a trooper."

"Hair?

"Short. Pixie cut."

"Colour?"

"Lavender. Purple is her signature colour."

Graham thundered out of the interview room and walked into his office, slamming the door behind him. He dialled a number.

"Mrs. Lampard? It's Detective Inspector Graham from Gorey Constabulary. I came to see you earlier."

He paused, "No nothing's wrong, I just have a couple of extra questions for you. Has anyone inquired about your room in the last few days?"

Mrs. Lampard spoke on the other end.

"I see, did she ask to see the room at all?" He waited as the elderly woman answered his question.

"And did you leave her alone?" Another pause.

"I'm sure it does, Mrs. Lampard. Well, thank you, that is all. You've been very helpful. Goodbye."

CHAPTER THIRTY-THREE

"THEY'VE GOT HER, sir. Boarding a flight to the mainland. They're bringing her in now," Harding said. Two immigration officers had intercepted Lillian Hart and handed her over to St. Helier police.

The doors were pushed open and Lillian, her mascara streaming and her lipstick smeared, jostled her way into the lobby between two bomber-jacketed policemen. Her hands were cuffed in front of her.

"This is outrageous!" she bellowed at Janice, who looked at her without batting an eyelid. Lillian saw Graham standing at the back of the office area, regarding her. "Are you in charge? I demand that I be released *immediately*!"

"Ms. Hart, if you don't calm down, you will be put into the cells until you do," Janice said. Graham hadn't moved, and she knew he had confidence in her to handle the prisoner.

"Don't be ridiculous."

"One more word, ma'am, and we'll put you in a cell," Janice repeated.

"Well, *really*." Janice booked Lillian in and took a DNA swab kit from a drawer under the desk. "Would you provide us with a DNA sample?"

"Is it really necessary?" Lillian objected, crossly.

"It is entirely voluntary at this stage, ma'am, but it will help our investigation." Lillian huffed but submitted, opening her mouth to allow Janice to wipe the swab around her mouth before she took her to the interview room. Graham continued to watch silently.

It took two hours for Ms. Hart's solicitor to arrive. During that time, she sat at the interview table or paced back and forth across the room. Periodically, she'd demand that she be allowed to smoke a cigarette and each time, Sergeant Harding who'd been given the task of guarding her, refused.

Eventually, everything was in place for the interview to start. Graham entered the room quietly, in marked contrast to the huffing woman. "I am Detective Inspector Graham, Ms. Hart."

"Why am I here?" Lillian almost shrieked. Her voice was shrill.

"You're here in connection with the murder of Felipe Barrios."

"You're being absurd. Do you know who I am?"

Graham ignored her. He lay a file on the table between them. "We understand that you flew in from the mainland three days ago? Can you tell me where you were on Wednesday night?"

"In my horrible boarding house, the White House Inn, trying to sleep despite all that clanking. Their heating system is simply appalling!

Graham suppressed a smile. He knew all about the "clanking." "Can anyone vouch for that?"

"I have no idea. You'll have to speak to the staff," Lillian responded.

"So if I spoke to Otto at reception, he'd tell me that he saw you go up to your room and that was all he saw of you until morning."

Lillian's head bobbed furiously. Graham's use of the White House Inn's reception manager's first name appeared to have unnerved her. "Of course," she said, a little uncertainty creeping into her voice.

"You see, Ms. Hart, we understand that your client, Ms. Hughes, asked you to call Mr. Barrios and attempt to buy an old family letter she was trying to locate. And, Ms. Hart, we have phone details that make a connection to Ms. Hughes *and* Mr. Barrios via a third party. Now would that third party be you, by any chance?"

"No."

"So this isn't you, then?" Graham placed Charlotte Hughes' phone on the table and played a voice message. Lillian's voice rang out.

"Charlotte, it's me. Where the hell are you? The fool wouldn't play ball. I'm going to try one more thing. Be in touch soon."

"This was placed shortly after a call from the same number was made to Felipe Barrios." Lillian pursed her lips and shut her eyes briefly. "I'm guessing that wasn't from you, either?"

"So what? All that proves is that I made a call." Lillian practically spat at him.

"Ms. Hughes has already told us that she was looking for an item that might be damaging to her family's reputation. What can you tell us about that?"

"Nothing, nothing at all. Charlotte told me she was worried and asked me to help her find it. I did call Mr. Barrios, but he told me he was completely unaware of such a thing." Lillian had transformed. Now she was smiling nervously, apparently eager to help but unable to do so.

"And you didn't go to Mr. Barrios' workshop later that evening?" Graham raised his eyebrows.

"No, why would I do that?"

"Perhaps to apply a little more pressure...?"

"Look, I demand you release me. I have done nothing wrong!"

"You see we found the weapon that killed Mr. Barrios in Don English's room..."

"Then why are you questioning me? It is he that should be sitting across the table from you. Not *me*."

"Except that he maintains his innocence."

Lillian scoffed, seizing the opportunity to go on the offensive again. "Well, what does that prove? He would, wouldn't he?" The door behind Lillian opened and Janice poked her head in. She flashed a thumbs up sign and quickly closed the door again.

"So when we examine your DNA and compare it with the evidence we found alongside the murder weapon, we won't find a match?"

"No." Lillian rubbed her nose. "How could you? I already said. I was in bed being kept awake in that infernal guest house."

"You're lying, Ms. Hart."

"No, I am not," Lillian was sitting up in her chair, rigid.

"I put it to you that you knew if this letter were exposed, it would cover your client in scandal, and therefore, you. Charlotte Hughes would risk losing the Parliamentary seat she is campaigning for. And you didn't want that, did you?"

"Are you suggesting I murdered a man all over some letter that may have harmed my *client's* reputation? That's preposterous. Of course it wasn't me. Murder? Me? Why would I do such a thing?"

"Because you thought you could get away with it. To protect your client. To protect yourself."

"Rubbish."

"Ms. Hart, we know you called Mr. Barrios to offer to buy the letter from him. We can also place you at Don English's B&B the day after the attack. I know for a fact that the reception desk is only manned at the White House Inn until midnight, so we only have your word for it that you were there all night. And we have a match for your DNA on hair found with the murder weapon. It's only a matter of time before we place you at the murder scene. Now tell me, are you sure you had nothing to do with the murder of Felipe Barrios?"

Lillian stared ahead, her mouth turned down, her eyelids half-closed. "Ms. Hart?"

Lillian pulled herself to her full height and exhaled. She looked at Graham defiantly. "Yes, yes, alright, I did it. The stupid man wouldn't take my money. I went there to persuade him. He wasn't supposed to *die*. I just wanted to knock him out so I could search for whatever it was I was looking for. And I *still* didn't find it."

"And you planted the murder weapon in Don English's room to frame him?"

Lillian sneered. "Don English is a *moron*. He'll never amount to anything. He'd be no loss to society." Her mouth pursed, an ugly plum streak. She held Graham's gaze, her back ramrod straight. "I did it for my client and her constituents. They are the losers in this."

"It's just marvellous, this," Roach enthused. He had travelled to the mainland to visit Dr. Oxley in his offices. "A few hours ago, this document was completely soaked with blood, but now..."

Oxley held the piece of paper aloft with a pair of tweezers. "Not bad," he conceded. "I've seen better, but this will do nicely. We have the author to thank, though." He set the document down in a plastic tray and slid it under the body of a machine that was so new it still had that 'new hardware smell.' At first glance, it appeared that a design team had become confused as to whether it was producing a flatbed scanner, a fax machine, or a high-end cappuccino maker.

"The author?" Roach asked. "How did he help?"

"Well," Oxley said, orienting the tray below a scanning arm and pressing a sequence of buttons on the machine's LCD display, "he used a type of ink which was pretty low in iron content. Blood naturally contains a good deal of iron, and old-fashioned common iron gall ink would have really confused matters. As it happens, we should be able to read the whole document once the X-ray scan is complete."

"Remarkable," Roach said. "How does it work?"

Twenty minutes later, Roach considered himself a minor expert on the use of X-ray technology to peer inside damaged and ancient documents. "So, even after it's been wet," he summarised, "the X-ray scan picks up the tiny rises in the contour of the paper caused by the impression of the pen, and the presence of the ink?"

"Spot on," Oxley said, relieved that Roach had a quicker and more agile mind than he had initially expected. "And, drum roll please..." The printer networked to the X-ray scanner began producing a high-resolution image, one fraction of an inch at a time, until the two men were virtually hopping from one foot to another with impatience.

"So, your boss," Oxley said as the print-out inched glacially along. "Smart chap, isn't he? Very deductive, I hear."

Roach didn't take his eyes off the emerging printout, as he replied, "As smart as they come. He's a detective, right down to his bones. Eats, sleeps, thinks, and breathes crime-solving. He's been very good to me."

Oxley nodded. "What do *you* think this is all about?" The letter was almost ready, but Oxley had already warned Roach against yanking it out of the printer prematurely.

"I think the letter was originally hidden in the desk," Roach said. "And I think it's going to fill in a lot of gaps in these cases we've been working on."

The printout dropped into the output tray and Oxley promptly picked it up. He turned it, so that they could read together. Three minutes later, as Roach dialled Graham's cellphone, Oxley said, "What are the chances that the person finding this would have the knowledge to know the significance of it?"

"Pretty tiny, I should imagine," Roach replied.

"Pity Mr. Barrios didn't turn this in right away. He might still be alive," Oxley said.

Graham picked up. Roach spoke seriously into his phone. "He was a traitor, sir. Sir Thomas Hughes. A traitor."

CHAPTER THIRTY-FOUR

The Palace of the People
Antigua de San Marcos
19 May, 1974

My dear Thomas,
 What a pleasure it is to write to you amidst the peace and quiet of a restful afternoon. You must be concerned about our wellbeing, but let me assure you that the recent unpleasantness is quite at an end. We are relaxing after a lengthy cabinet meeting this morning—Julia sends her kisses, both to you and Susannah, whom we hope is very well. I'm sure she is as beautiful as ever.

Perhaps I should revise my greeting, above—it is Sir Thomas now, is it not? Congratulations on this long overdue honour; finally, your imperialist Queen has seen fit to elevate you as you deserve, some twenty months after San Marcos bestowed her highest award upon our most loyal European friend. It is no less than you deserve.

It is out of friendship that I write today, Sir Thomas. Words cannot express the great debt that is now owed to you *by the freedom-loving people of San Marcos. I say this only to you, as I am certain of your discretion. We were staring into the abyss, my friend. The rebels were rampaging through the countryside, looting and burning. Even my military commanders were beginning to plan for the worst. There was talk of a massive barricade around the city. Without proper intelligence or air power, the advance would never have been stopped, and we could not long have endured a siege.*

But then, the angels came in the form of you! Long moribund and gathering dust at our three aerodromes, our helicopters, refitted thanks to your kindness, took to the skies and saved the revolution! I begged our neighbours, our friends, even the KGB, for the spare parts to bring our air forces back to life, but only you responded. You recognised the danger, and you took swift and decisive action. And for this timely response, I owe you my presidency and the future security and happiness of my country as well as my life and those of my family.

Please be assured of my complete and utter discretion. I am indeed aware of the jeopardy you put yourself in to help us, and the danger to you should your role on our behalf become known. I realise you will be seen as an Enemy of your People. This is not a debt easily repaid, Sir Thomas, but I will find a way. Please know that, should it become necessary, there will always be a home for you here. In the meantime, the people of San Marcos owe you the deepest and most profound thanks. I will forever hold you in the very highest esteem. You have my own deepest and sincerest thanks, as well as my fond and lifelong friendship.

Your loyal and grateful brother,
General Augusto Fuente
President of San Marcos

CHAPTER THIRTY-FIVE

THE RULES WERE firm and clear. Graham knew he couldn't close his office door during this delicate interview with Laura Beecham. Instead, the intensely curious, but assiduously toiling Sergeant Harding and Constable Roach would be able to witness much of the meeting from the open-plan office outside his own. Graham was determined that it appear as professional as possible.

"I know I promised coffee," Graham said, "but in truth, I'm much more of a tea man."

Sitting across from him, in dark jeans and a grey sweater, Laura bit her lip anxiously. Her first scheduled encounter with this attractive, interesting man was taking place, not at a coffee or tea shop as they had planned, but at a police station. In his office, no less. And as part of an investigation that had yielded the arrest of a man wanted for multiple murders.

"Mrs. Taylor did warn me," she said. "What type of tea are you treating me to?"

Graham could tell by the scent of the leaves, without even checking the container. "Jasmine from Taiwan," he said. "Very aromatic, just a little floral. Full of antioxidants too, so they claim. Apparently it can help people recovering from serious illness."

Laura gave him a small smile. "Well, I'm recovering from a bit of a shock, I'll admit, but I have you to thank that it wasn't more serious. That gunman could have killed me."

Graham sipped his tea and began making notes. "I can't take any credit, I'm afraid, much as I'd like to. Constable Barnwell was your saviour, not me. I was wrapped up in a murder case. I didn't know anything about it until it was all over.

Laura brushed this off. "You can't be everywhere. And your constable was magnificent."

"I'll make sure he knows that," Graham said. "But I have to ask, Miss Beecham..."

"Laura," she said. "Please."

"I have to ask, Laura, why would a notorious mob figure like Frank Bertolli come down to Jersey to kill you?" Graham had spent a significant part of the last hours developing several theories, but each was less credible than the last. Laura was not the type to have become involved in any criminal activity; at least Graham *hoped* she wasn't. Though he'd have said the same thing about Don English, Adam Harris-Watts, and perhaps even Charlotte Hughes. Lillian Hart, on the other hand, was an aberration that couldn't be anticipated.

"Okay, but this must all remain 'off the record,'" Laura said leaning forward and lowering her voice. "That has to be a condition of my explaining it."

Graham closed his notebook and pushed it away. "No problem."

"And," she asked, turning to glance behind her, "could we close the door?"

"It's against the rules," Graham explained, "without another officer present."

"Just for a few moments," Laura requested. "I want to make sure this isn't overheard."

Graham hesitated, then moved to close the door. He thought he caught the tail end of Harding and Roach ducking their heads, but they appeared to be working with an uncommon focus. He sat back down and allowed Laura to tell her story in her own way.

She exhaled and began. "I was working in a pub just by Stratford Station in east London." She gave him a quick smile to hide her embarrassment. "A librarian's pay isn't enough to live on in London, that's for sure. Do you know the area?"

"Vaguely. Where the Olympic Park is?"

"Right. Well, there was a group of men who came in regularly. Over a few weeks we got friendly, you know, them telling me their problems, troubles at home, or at work, just banter, typical stuff," she shrugged.

Graham nodded. "Go on."

"Well, one Sunday night, they came in quite late and in a good mood. The landlord stayed open after closing time and asked me to stay on to serve them. It was just them and me. I thought they'd come from a football game or maybe the dog track. They were buying champagne and cocktails. It was out of character."

Arms folded, Graham leant back and pictured the scene. "So what were they celebrating? A win on the dogs?"

Laura looked over her shoulder just once to make sure the door was closed. "A diamond heist. One of the biggest. Diamonds worth a hundred million pounds."

Graham couldn't prevent his mouth from falling open. "The Marble-Kilgore heist?" he gasped. "They *admitted* it?"

"Not in so many words," Laura cautioned. "But I overheard enough of what they said. I went to the police and agreed to become a witness, but…"

"You needed protecting. And what better way than to spirit you off to a quiet little island in the English Channel?"

Laura nodded and tucked a strand of blonde hair behind her ear. "Exactly. The Met wanted it kept as quiet as possible."

"So quiet," Graham pointed out, his eyebrows raised, "that they didn't even tell Jersey Police about you."

Laura frowned, "The officer in charge of the witness protection scheme said that…"

"Someone down here might blab," Graham said. "Sensible enough, I suppose, though a little over-cautious. Besides," he added with just a hint of frustration, "if we'd known you were here, *we* could have protected you."

Laura gave a long sigh. "I recognise that now. If I had the time over, I'd do things differently." She looked at him apologetically.

"It wasn't your fault." Graham met her gaze. "Thank you for levelling with me. I have to admit the whole thing had me rather stumped."

Laura feigned surprise. "The legendary DI Graham, *stumped*? Surely not."

He let his professional demeanour drop a little. "Well," he grinned sheepishly, "only for a few hours. But still, if you *hadn't* come down here, we wouldn't have collared Bertolli."

"And we would never have met," Laura pointed out.

There were ten seconds of silence before Graham found the courage to dispense with the rules for the second time in almost as many minutes and say what he most wanted to. "You know, I'm actually due half a day off."

"And the library is closed for repairs." Laura said, smiling.

Graham stood. "I wonder if you would allow me to show you around the island. Maybe take you to some of the sights?" He made a fuss of opening the door and was gratified to find Roach and Harding once more silently intent upon their work. "Any calls come in, Sergeant?" he asked Harding.

"Nothing we can't handle, sir," she replied. "Taking a half-day, sir?"

He shot her a look but only briefly. "I think I will," he said.

"We all deserve a break, I reckon," Constable Roach piped up. "We've had quite enough excitement for a while. And, I've got my sergeant's exam in ten days.'"

"Ten days?! High time for a quiz then, wouldn't you say?" Harding bustled around, getting down the police duties manual.

There was a bang, and they all turned to see Constable Barnwell burst through the doors.

"Mornin' all. How are we doin'?" Barnwell noticed Graham shrugging into his jacket. "On your way out, sir?"

"Yes, Constable," Graham said in a tone that didn't invite further questioning. "Whilst I'm gone, sort that room out in the back. It's like Piccadilly Circus in there."

Graham and Laura left them to it and headed out into the spring sunshine. "Where first?" Laura asked. "I haven't been to the castle yet."

Graham smiled knowingly. "Let me give Stephen Jeffries a call. The exhibit hasn't opened yet, but there are some displays in the basement that you won't *believe*." He dialled Jeffries number. "Ready?" he asked.

Laura gave him a smile that matched the sunny day. "Ready."

EPILOGUE

THE FALL FROM grace experienced by Charlotte Hughes and her campaign manager, Lillian Hart, in the days after their arrests was swift and absolute as knowledge of Sir Thomas Hughes' treasonous activities became known.

Charlotte Hughes was charged with attempting to pervert the course of justice and was sentenced to 300 hours of community service. She completed it by working on a rundown, drug-riddled estate in Goslingdale. Her tasks included picking up litter, cleaning off graffiti, clearing wasteland, and maintaining community property, all whilst wearing a distinctive orange vest.

Lillian Hart was sentenced to fifteen years in prison for the voluntary manslaughter of **Felipe Barrios**. She appealed her sentence and requested a move to an open women's prison, but her appeal was rejected. She has received no visitors during her imprisonment thus far and has no expectation of any in the future. She was offered the chance to learn woodworking during her stay in prison but turned it down.

Don English was found guilty of three crimes, including breaking and entering and perverting the course of justice. A charge of involuntary manslaughter in the case of Charles Norris's death could not be proven. He was given a sentence of six months jail time and two years community service. He served three months in HMP Shrewsbury and later found work as a gardener working in the grounds of a National Trust property. He still lives in Goslingdale.

The Hughes' family solicitor, **Carl Prendergast**, was a witness in all three cases. In a statement to the press, he claimed that he "would prefer to have nothing more to do with the Hughes family. Spending decades dealing with one dreadful, sociopathic Hughes was quite enough." A week before Charlotte Hughes' trial began, he announced his retirement from practicing law.

Adam Harris-Watts was sacked from his position as curator of the Jersey Heritage Museum. He was sentenced to 75 hours community service and now works as a researcher for a left-wing academic at Manchester University.

. . .

Frank Bertolli was sentenced to twelve years for the attempted murder of Laura Beecham and Billy Foster. He also asked for six other murder charges to be taken into consideration. He is likely to die in jail unless he is willing to turn Queen's evidence against those who hired him.

Thomas Hughes' estate gave permission for the Fuente letter to be published as part of a full-page London Times advertisement that began an international campaign to seek justice for those mistreated or executed by Fuente's government. The raising of awareness and important celebrity endorsements led to mounting and eventually intolerable pressure on the crumbling regime. Within a year, a peaceful revolution swept the now elderly general from power. San Marcos recently held its first democratic elections since the early 1970s.

Shortly after the arrests of Don English, Lillian Hart, Adam Harris-Watts, Charlotte Hughes, and Frank Bertolli, **Janice Harding and Jack Wentworth** took five days holiday to drive around southern France. On their return, they began looking for an apartment together in Gorey.

Barry Barnwell was once again commended for his valiant and selfless efforts and received a second Queen's Gallantry Medal at Buckingham Palace. He was offered a much higher profile assignment by the Metropolitan Police, one his London-based mother hoped he'd accept, but he turned it down.

. . .

Near perfect results in his sergeant's exam and a glowing recommendation from DI David Graham brought a new opportunity for **Constable Jim Roach**. He will divide his time between Gorey and the forensics lab in St. Helier, where he will study criminology and pathology under the guidance of **Dr. Marcus Tomlinson.**

After the case, **Simon Oxley** resumed his semester of teaching at Cambridge University. He recently published a paper in *X-ray Quarterly* discussing his role in decoding "THE LETTER".

Viv Foster was accepted into Jersey's drug rehabilitation program once again and is doing well. **Billy** visits her daily. On Sergeant Harding's recommendation, Social Services fostered Billy with Mrs. Lampard for the duration of Viv's stay in the program, giving Billy a stable home base on the island and Mrs. Lampard some company and a regular income. Despite their disparate ages, the two get on famously. As Billy had generally refused to talk about it and was not required to testify at the trial, the incident at the library remains shrouded in mystery among his peers. Harding and Barnwell did, however, refer to Billy as a "hero" during a visit to his school recently, something which has completely transformed his school life.

. . .

David Graham and Laura Beecham are often seen together at the Bangkok Palace for their regular Friday "date night." She always has the Pad Thai or Tom Yum soup whilst he always experiments with whatever's hottest on the menu. The waiting staff no longer ask him to confirm his well-being the morning afterward.

Thank you for reading *The Case of the Missing Letter*! I hope you love Inspector Graham and his gang as much as I do. The next book in the Inspector David Graham series continues with a new case that features a missing scientist, a dark and stormy night, a secret worth killing for...

As the clues and motives pile up, Graham is forced to cancel yet another date. A crime this diabolical takes teamwork to solve, and the inspector enlists the aid of his three loyal and beloved officers. But are four heads really better than one?

Only a single thing is certain; a killer still lurks off Jersey's windswept shores. And if Graham and his team can't apprehend the culprit soon, the Inspector's love life may be the next victim... Get your copy of The Case of the Pretty Lady from Amazon now! The Case of the Pretty Lady is FREE in Kindle Unlimited.

To find out about new books, sign up for my newsletter: https://www.alisongolden.com.

If you love the Inspector Graham mysteries, you'll also love the sweet, funny *USA Today* bestselling Reverend Annabelle Dixon series featuring a madcap, lovable lady vicar whose passion for cake is matched only by her desire for justice. The first in the series, *Death at the Cafe* is available for purchase from Amazon. Like all my books, *Death at the Cafe* is FREE in Kindle Unlimited.

And don't miss the Roxy Reinhardt mysteries. Will Roxy triumph after her life falls apart? She's sacked from her job, her boyfriend dumps her, she's out of money. So, on a whim, she goes on the trip of a lifetime to New Orleans, There, she gets mixed up in a Mardi Gras murder. *Things were going to be fine. They were, weren't they?* Get the first in the series, Mardi Gras Madness from Amazon. Also FREE in Kindle Unlimited!

If you're looking for something edgy and dangerous, root for Diana Hunter as she seeks justice after a devastating crime destroys her family. Start following her journey in this non-stop series of suspense and action. The first book in the series, Snatched is available to buy on Amazon and is FREE in Kindle Unlimited.

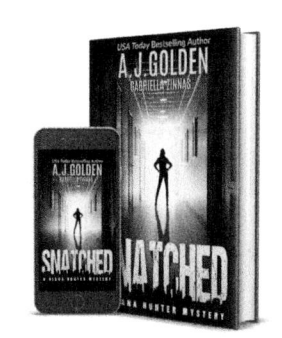

I hugely appreciate your help in spreading the word about *The Case of the Missing Letter*, including telling a friend. Reviews help readers find books! Please leave a review on your favourite book site.

Turn the page for an excerpt from sixth book in the Inspector Graham series, *The Case of the Pretty Lady*...

ALISON GOLDEN
Grace Dagnall

USA Today Bestselling Author

Mussels Not Brussels

AN INSPECTOR DAVID GRAHAM MYSTERY

The Case of the
Pretty
Lady

THE CASE OF THE PRETTY LADY
CHAPTER ONE

EVEN BEFORE THEY heard him speak, his bulk, the brilliantly white Stetson, and his endearing manner marked him as an American tourist. "You know what I'm wondering?" the man boomed in a Texan drawl. "I'm wondering what on the good Lord's earth a *fo'c'sle* is." He pronounced it "fock-slee," to the amusement of the early lunchtime crowd. "Anyone want to educate a newcomer?" he asked the two-thirds empty bar.

The barman, Lewis Hurd had this covered and not for the first time. "A 'forecastle'," he explained. "It's the front part of the deck of a working ship or a warship."

"You don't say," the American replied. "And how the heck do you pronounce it?"

The regulars at the bar replied in an oft-rehearsed chorus. "Fock-sul."

"Awesome," the American beamed. "But what's a *ferret* doing on a *warship*?"

Hurd leant in to handle this one whilst the pub's patrons, here for the dependable grub or to enjoy the hand-crafted ales alongside like-minded souls, returned to their conversations.

Over in the corner, an invective of French rose into the air, followed by a roar of approval. Five men in boots and work overalls stood talking over one another as they drank their pints. One man poked a finger at another who gesticulated rapidly as he defended himself against some unknown accusation. The ferocity of their discussion would have seemed threatening were it not for the smiles on the faces of their countrymen. Soon words gave way to back thumps and clinking glasses, gestures that told other pub-goers that all was well.

Lewis Hurd looked at the group, barely concealed dislike curling his lip. "Keep your voices down, lads, please," he called over, his words more reasonable than the feelings his expression conveyed.

Beyond them, by the big, paned windows with their view of the harbour, Tamsin Porter and Greg Somerville, two thirty-somethings, fit and trim in their high-end outdoor wear, were sitting in sullen silence, refusing to even look at one another. Tamsin stared into her half-finished pint, her hands fiddling with the cord that circled the perimeter of her jacket's hood whilst Greg let his gaze wander over the masts of the boats in the harbour and the members of a crew who chatted as they sheltered from a sudden downpour beneath a barely sufficient awning.

"So, you're not going to say anything?" Tamsin asked, finally.

Greg sighed, the momentary peace brought to an unwelcome end. "What do you want me to say, Tamsin?"

"I don't know. Something. Anything."

"Shall I stand up, right here," he proposed, "and admit

to the whole pub that I'm a poor scientist? Would that do you?"

"Greg, come on..."

"Or that I'm an unreliable partner, that I can't source enough funding for more robust trackers, and therefore my data can't be trusted?" His temper rose quickly, along with his voice. "That I should have found a way to become clairvoyant and *predicted* that our work might be interrupted by a freak storm?"

Tamsin pushed her pint away and folded her arms. "Calm down, all right?"

"I can't stand to hear you complain about my anger when you're the one who does the most to create it. Why don't you stop criticising and *help* for once?"

Their relationship, once admired by their friends for its stability and endurance, was in a strange, disappointing, some might say vicious spiral. They didn't talk any more. They just argued and nit-picked and called each other terrible names, only to apologise the next day, and begin the acrimony all over again, the day after that.

"We're going to get some good data," Greg promised. "They're coming in, maybe eight or ten of them, and if one comes anywhere near a buoy, we'll pick up the UHF signal, and we'll know *exactly* where our little beauties are travelling to."

"*If* the hurricane doesn't shift their behaviour patterns," Tamsin countered.

The rotund American was still wandering around the pub, drink firmly in hand, examining the photos and old examples of fishing gear nailed to the walls. "Tell me, are you guys from out of town, too?" he asked them cheerily, oblivious to the tension simmering between the couple.

Tamsin made no move to even look up, but Greg was

glad of the distraction. "We are, but we're working here," he said.

"On what?" the American asked.

Tamsin turned, her eyes tired and still a little swollen from crying earlier. She said simply, "Sharks."

The American's eyes widened, a reaction the couple was used to. "Get outta here," he breathed. "What do you do?"

"We're marine biologists. We're involved in a British government project to track the population of Holden Sharks. This is our third year tracking them."

"Huh!" It was that curious, open-minded sound that meant, "Say more about that."

"They migrate through the English Channel, but no one's proven where they go to breed. We're here to gather that data."

"Neat!" the American exclaimed. "I've never heard of a...what're they called, again?"

Greg folded his arms. "Holden sharks. They're among the rarest in the world," he explained. "Little bit like a basking shark," he added, pointing to a photo on the wall which showed the giant, unlikely animal approaching the camera, its jaw cranked open to reveal not teeth, but rows of fleshy filters, like those of a whale. "And they head through here on their way to the Norwegian Sea, where they mate, feed, and then head back toward the open Atlantic."

"At least," Tamsin interrupted, her fingertip pressing the table in a sudden rush of frustration. "We *think* that's what they do. Opinions vary." She gave Greg a sideways glance, the now-obvious, strange, electric tension between the pair telling the American visitor that the theory was a major bone of contention between them. "We need the data from our buoys to support any conclusions. It may be that they simply turn around here for some reason and head straight back out."

Greg wouldn't let this go. "That's highly unlikely and you know it," he said, well aware that they were restarting a two-year-old argument in front of a bemused layman. "Sharks don't do one-eighties unless they're lost."

"What about those whale sharks in the Gulf of Thailand?" Tamsin argued. "They swam up there and turned right around."

The American nodded politely to them both and wandered off, unwilling to be neither enabling party, nor participant, in this increasingly bitter confrontation.

"Case in point," Greg retorted. "They were lost and corrected their path."

Before Tamsin could compose a counterpoint, the swing door next to them burst open and a man walked in, shaking himself dry. The moisture from his waterproofs caught the light in the dim, dingy bar as drips tracked his movements on the floor.

Surprised, Tamsin and Greg looked up, Greg immediately stiffening whilst Tamsin resumed fingering her hood's drawstring. When he caught sight of them, the man's eyes widened with shock, but he took a step toward them, his hand extended.

"Tamsin, Greg," he acknowledged, looking at them in turn.

"Kev, what're you doing here?" Greg ignored the outstretched hand, but Tamsin filled the uncomfortable void and shook it.

"Just came in out of the rain."

"Not here, *here*. On Jersey. You're not following us again, are you? You know we have a permit, right? And government funding."

"Yeah, I heard." Kev sounded like he'd heard it more than once, too.

Greg half-rose from the bench he was sitting on, his anger along with the volume of his voice increasing again. "Listen, you have no right..."

"Greg..." Tamsin put a warning hand on his arm, and Greg wavered. He sat down again, catching sight of Lewis Hurd carefully watching the trio as he slowly polished a glass behind the varnished, wooden bar.

"Be on your way, Kev. We better not see you out on the water, okay?" she said.

"Nice to see you, too. " The man shrugged and sidled off, dragging from his head the woollen beanie that held his bushy hair in check and brushing drops from his beard.

Greg shook his head. "That's all we need. Another animal rights pain in the bum. If you want to complain about someone, Tamsin, complain about them. Why don't they do their homework and understand that what we do will sustain the herd, not threaten them?"

Greg stood suddenly, forcefully enough to jar the table. The warming remains of Tamsin's pint wobbled dangerously. She moved to steady it.

"The weather's fairing up," he told her, "and I'm due out to collect the in-situ data from the buoys. This might be the last time for a few days given the forecast. You can come with me, or sit here and continue telling the whole pub what a rubbish scientist I am." He grabbed his jacket. "It's entirely up to you." Greg stomped out of the bar and up the stairs to the room they'd been sharing above the pub, leaving Tamsin feeling hollow and strangely abandoned.

Lewis Hurd sidled over to collect Greg's empty mug and returned to the bar silently. Tamsin continued to stare at her drink, but as she pushed it away, she saw Greg leave the pub and watched him out of the window heading down to his small motor launch, wondering what had happened to the fun, loving relationship they'd once had. And also wondering just how long the strained, combative one that had replaced it could possibly last.

Greg could see the damage from a quarter mile away through his powerful binoculars. "Damn it," he cursed as he applied the left rudder, bringing his small boat gradually alongside the cracked, orange buoy. Sixteen of the buoys, arranged in a pattern between the Portland and Thames sea areas, were intended to give Greg and Tamsin the clearest picture yet of Holden shark movements in the Channel. But this one would never transmit again. The bright orange chassis had split, exposing the buoy's electronic innards to the raging sea. The wind was getting up, and Greg cursed again as he struggled to winch the buoy on board. "How did this happen?"

He sat down in the boat as he examined the buoy. He felt emotionally drained. The constant arguing with Tamsin was wearing on his nerves, and as he'd prepared to leave the harbour earlier, he'd been heckled by a couple of locals. The fishermen resented their presence every year, although there was no evidence to suggest that their methods for collecting data affected the fishermen or their catch at all. The sight of Kev Cummings in the pub had just added to his troubles. Kev was the regional director of the local SeaWatch chapter, a grand title for someone who was, in Greg's opinion, a simple yob. Their annual game of "cat and mouse" was a complication he found tiresome. It was exhausting to be the villain when all you were doing was your best to protect the marine ecosystem, ultimately for everyone's benefit. *If only they could see that.*

Greg frowned at the mess of salt-corroded wires, so bent and misshapen as to be almost unrecognisable. Two wires twisted impotently in the air. The ends were clean cut. Greg stood, feet apart, in the gently swaying boat, the buoy lying easily in his hands as he stared at the horizon. His eyes darkened as his fury built once more. The impending poor weather had driven seafarers ashore early and sidelined the commercial vessels transporting tourists seeking cheap booze from the coastal French hypermarkets. Greg looked around. With the exception of one boat some distance away, he was alone on the water.

He put the buoy aside and set course for the next one. In theory, each time a shark passed by the buoy's receptors, the tiny transponders within the shark's skin would activate, transmitting a long-term record of the animal's depth, speed, and course. Although sharks turned suddenly for all kinds of reasons, Greg's thesis was that they were migrating generally *east*, and that they ultimately emerged in the North Sea where they patrolled off the coast of Norway as they waited for potential mates to arrive. His data would settle long-standing questions about shark behaviour and perhaps help to raise money and awareness for shark conservation. *Jaws* had done enduring harm to the reputation and safety of sharks all over the world, and Greg felt a moral duty to do his part in reversing some worrying trends.

Not everyone saw his research like that, however. Animal activists were a constant irritant to marine biologists. Some felt the moral imperative was to leave the sharks entirely alone, to allow them to continue their natural behaviour, honed over centuries, unencumbered by man's efforts to understand them. Others believed that any study was bound to disrupt the animals, provide false data, and even threaten their existence.

Greg found the activists to be largely wilful, illogical, and uneducated in the ways of the animals they claimed to be trying to protect. As far as he was concerned, they romanticised the sharks and imagined the threat posed by his research. Thankfully, they usually went no further than making their presence felt on land in low-key ways; they would hang around the launch site or "bump" into him and Tamsin around town. Neither of them felt particularly intimidated, nor did the activists seek to intervene directly in their work. This new possibility that his research was being actively sabotaged represented a significantly increased level of intimidation, one that was concerning, and most definitely dangerous to the sharks. Even perhaps himself.

Greg's next buoy lay a mile away, Day-Glo orange and gratifyingly upright. Like an iceberg, the waves concealed much of its mass. Below the surface, a weighty ballast kept the buoy steady whilst the orange tower above helped fend off collisions in these busy sea lanes. Greg pulled alongside and reached over to open a panel and slot in a cable. He then waited the requisite ten seconds with his fingers crossed, and checked his phone for the data flow. "Green across the board. Sweet."

Only after he'd returned to the boat's modest pilot house and given the data a cursory examination did he see the good news: *six* Holden sharks had come through over the past three days. Forgetting his earlier concerns, he slapped the boat's wheel and hooted. "Yes!"

Preoccupied with jubilation, he sensed nothing untoward until there was an unexpected noise behind him, sudden and firm, as though something large had collided hard with the stern of his boat. Greg was thrown forward hard onto his hands and knees and shook his head roughly as the sound of feet landing on the deck of his motor launch reached his ears.

To get your copy of *The Case of the Pretty Lady*, visit the link below:

https://www.alisongolden.com/pretty-lady

"Your emails seem to come on days when I need to read them because they are so upbeat."
- Linda W -

For a limited time, you can get the first books in each of my series - *Chaos in Cambridge, Hunted* (exclusively for subscribers - not available anywhere else), *The Case of the Screaming Beauty, and Mardi Gras Madness* - plus updates about new releases, promotions, and other Insider exclusives, by signing up for my mailing list at:

https://www.alisongolden.com/graham

TAKE MY QUIZ

What kind of mystery reader are you? Take my thirty second quiz to find out!

https://www.alisongolden.com/quiz

BOOKS IN THE INSPECTOR DAVID GRAHAM SERIES

The Case of the Screaming Beauty

The Case of the Hidden Flame

The Case of the Fallen Hero

The Case of the Broken Doll

The Case of the Missing Letter

The Case of the Pretty Lady

The Case of the Forsaken Child

The Case of Sampson's Leap

The Case of the Uncommon Witness

COLLECTIONS

Books 1-4

The Case of the Screaming Beauty

The Case of the Hidden Flame

The Case of the Fallen Hero

The Case of the Broken Doll

Books 5-7

The Case of the Missing Letter

The Case of the Pretty Lady

The Case of the Forsaken Child

ALSO BY ALISON GOLDEN

FEATURING REVEREND ANNABELLE DIXON
Chaos in Cambridge (Prequel)

Death at the Café

Murder at the Mansion

Body in the Woods

Grave in the Garage

Horror in the Highlands

Killer at the Cult

Fireworks in France

Witches at the Wedding

FEATURING ROXY REINHARDT
Mardi Gras Madness

New Orleans Nightmare

Louisiana Lies

Cajun Catastrophe

As A. J. Golden
FEATURING DIANA HUNTER
Hunted (Prequel)

Snatched

Stolen

Chopped

Exposed

ABOUT THE AUTHOR

Alison Golden is the *USA Today* bestselling author of the Inspector David Graham mysteries, a traditional British detective series, and two cozy mystery series featuring main characters Reverend Annabelle Dixon and Roxy Reinhardt. As A. J. Golden, she writes the Diana Hunter thriller series.

Alison was raised in Bedfordshire, England. Her aim is to write stories that are designed to entertain, amuse, and calm. Her approach is to combine creative ideas with excellent writing and edit, edit, edit. Alison's mission is simple: To write excellent books that have readers clamouring for more.

Alison is based in the San Francisco Bay Area with her husband and twin sons. She splits her time between London and San Francisco.

For up-to-date promotions and release dates of upcoming books, sign up for the latest news here: https://www.alisongolden.com/graham.

For more information:
www.alisongolden.com
alison@alisongolden.com

- facebook.com/alisongolden.books
- x.com/alisonjgolden
- instagram.com/alisonjgolden

THANK YOU

Thank you for taking the time to read *The Case of the Missing Letter*. If you enjoyed it, please consider telling your friends or posting a short review. Word of mouth is an author's best friend and very much appreciated.

Thank you,

Printed in Great Britain
by Amazon